CONTENTS

EMILY SHADOW-HUNTER 6 DOMINATION

CHAPTER 1

Yelena looked at the Grinder with utter contempt. 'How can you be sure he has tracked down the Daywalker?' she asked.

Igor shrugged, his massively overdeveloped shoulders shifting under his suit like human tectonic plates. 'Can't,' he admitted. 'That's why I sent one of the familiars to check. A couple of simple questions and we shall have our confirmation.'

Iscat the Grinder started howling as he attempted to break free of the binds Igor had restrained him with. Igor punched him in the neck to shut him up and the creature whimpered into silence.

A few minutes later, the familiar returned and got into the vampire's blacked-out SUV.

'Report,' commanded Yelena.

'They were here,' stated the ex-Spetsnaz member. 'A tall blonde. Looks like a fashion model. Three men with her. All large. The man on duty describes them as, scary.'

'You say, were?'

'Yes,' confirmed the familiar. 'They left not two hours ago. The reception says when they left, two old men joined the group.'

'Where were they heading?'

The familiar shook his head. 'No one has any idea. Sorry.'

'Fine,' said Yelena. 'Return to your vehicle. Igor will get the Seeker to find them. Two hours is not much of a head start. We are getting close.'

The monster vamp smiled. An awful sight to behold.

CHAPTER 2

'Can we stop for French stew with some of that long bread?' asked Tag. 'I'm starving.'

'Sure,' answered Troy. 'As soon as we get out of Paris. I could do with some grub as well.'

'You literally ate just before we left,' noted Emily.

'True,' agreed Troy. 'But it was a rushed snack, because Merlin was so insistent that we get going.'

'You had three steak sandwiches,' argued Emily. 'Tag had four.'

'I do not recommend stopping,' interjected the Prof.

'Why?' asked Emily.

'We are being followed.'

Merlin turned to face the Fae Professor. 'Already? How can she have gotten on to us so quickly?'

The Prof shook his head. 'Not her,' he replied. 'Someone else. Can't you feel it?'

Merlin closed his eyes and concentrated for a few seconds, then he let out a heavy sigh. 'Yes,' he affirmed. 'Of course. Damn it, how could I have missed that?'

'Easy,' said the Prof. 'It's because they are not using a spell. There is no overt magic involved, but whatever it is, there is a certain amount of unnatural feeling about it. I am not sure what it is.'

No one spoke as they allowed the Prof and the wizard to think.

'Not human,' ventured Merlin.

'Definitely not,' concurred the Prof. 'Almost animal.'

Again, Merlin closed his eyes. 'Got it,' he exclaimed. 'It's a Seeker. I remember that signature from the Arthurian wars.'

'A Seeker?' asked Emily.

'It's a *Nosferatu* anomaly,' explained the Prof. 'Usually a Grinder that has randomly developed the skill while being turned. They develop the ability to track a target across oceans if need be. Fortunately, as they are so phenomenally dim witted, they are relatively easy to fool.'

'How?' asked Emily.

Merlin grinned and wiggled his fingers. 'Magic,' he said. 'I shall create a false path for them to follow. Lead them in a different direction.'

'That will work?' asked Emily.

'Merlin shrugged. 'Probably. What worries me is why they are looking for us, and who are they?'

'How will we know if it has worked?' asked Troy.

'Well, I suppose we'll know when whoever they are stop following us,' replied Merlin.

'Cool,' said Tag. 'Then can we stop for stew?'

Emily rolled her eyes, and Merlin didn't deign to answer.

Instead, both Merlin and the Prof sat down at

the table in the rear of the campervan. The Prof took out a roll of parchment from his ever-present leather case and Merlin appeared to pluck a pair feathered quills and a pot of ink from thin air.

Then the two of them proceeded to scratch hundreds of tiny designs on the parchment, seemingly at random. Some of Merlin's runes and shapes overlapped the Prof's and many of the Prof's were so tiny they looked like little more than slightly blurred dots.

Even when the vehicle hit a pothole and bounced rather alarmingly on its enhanced suspension, neither of the ancients missed a beat, their respective quills pausing only to be dipped into the ink and then returning to the parchment.

Emily, Troy and Tag watched closely for almost ten minutes; the strange writings being fashioned proving to be almost hypnotic in their production.

Muller, who was driving, kept his eyes on the road.

Tag was the first one to lose interest and he got up and went to sit in the passenger seat next to the Knight.

'What's happening back there?' asked Muller.

'The two old men are writing loads of stuff on a piece of paper,' answered Tag. 'Meanwhile, Tag is starving to death. It be inhumane.'

Muller reached down, flipped open a storage compartment and took out a large packet of what looked like jerky. He flicked it at Tag who caught in with one hand.

11

'What's this?'

'Smoked Andouillette sausage,' answered Muller. 'It's a French specialty.'

Tag peered suspiciously at the dried sausage. Then he opened the bag. An awful smell wafted out.

'Man, this sausage is off,' he said as he twisted the bag shut.

Muller shook his head. 'No, it just smells like that. Trust me, it's fine.'

Tag cracked the bag open and took another smell. 'No ways. Smells like crap. What's it taste like?'

Muller thought for a few seconds before he answered. 'Honestly? Must admit, tastes a bit funky.'

Tag frowned. 'Well why you buy it then?'

Muller shrugged. 'It's an acquired taste. Try some, it's not so bad once you get past the smell. And the taste.'

Tag opened the window and threw the bag out.

'Hey,' yelled Muller. 'That stuff isn't cheap.'

'Bloody French,' mumbled Tag. 'Snails and Frog's legs and fish eggs and stinky crappy sausage.'

No one spoke as Merlin and the Prof continued their scratching. After another twenty minutes, the parchment began to glow with a bright yellow light. Both of the men began to chant softly under their breaths as they carried on sketching. A high-pitched whine filled the air, like a finger running along the rim of a crystal glass.

The light brightened and then, with a flash, the

scroll disappeared.

Both Merlin and the Prof sank back in their seats, sweat pouring down their faces.

'It is done,' said Merlin. 'We have sent them on a merry goose chase.' The wizard allowed himself a small smile. 'And I think they will be suitably un-enthusiastic with the outcome.'

'Excellent,' said Tag. 'Can we stop for stew now?'

'Tag,' said Merlin wearily.

'Yep?'

'Shut up.'

The vehicle continued down the highway, heading out of Paris and towards Merlin's mountain hideout, some five hundred miles away.

CHAPTER 3

The two SUV's bumped down the rough track, driving deeper into the rugged countryside that made up the Pyrenees region of Southern France.

The Chernobyl vampires, their pet Grinder and a familiar driver were on point in their fully blacked out vehicle. The Spetsnaz familiars took up the rear, following the Seeker's directions.

Then the rear vehicle flashed its lights and pulled over. The lead car followed suite while the ranking Spetsnaz member leaped out, jogged to the vampire's vehicle and got in.

'What?' snapped Yelena.

The familiar was an ex-Spetsnaz operative named Timofey Cherny, but all called him *Starshyna*, which was short for Senior Sergeant. 'I know this road, mistress,' he answered.

'So?'

'It leads to a place called, The Farm,' continued *Starshyna*.

'This had better have some relevance to our search,' said Yelena. 'Because I do not take well to time wasting.'

'The Farm is a nickname that the troops have

given this place,' explained *Starshyna*. 'It is where they are trained.'

'Who?'

'The *Légion étrangère*,' answered the familiar. 'The French Foreign Legion.'

'Why would the Daywalker be visiting the Legion?' queried Igor.

Starshyna shrugged. 'I have no idea, Master,' he answered. 'But I do know one thing. We need to display some caution.'

Yelena sneered at the Spetsnaz veteran. 'Why?' she questioned. 'Are you afraid of them?'

Starshyna looked at the hideously deformed super-vamp. His gaze was steady. Calm. Accepting.

He nodded. 'Yes, mistress,' he admitted. 'The Legion have a saying - *Honneur et Fidélité pericula ludus ad unum.*'

'I have never bothered to speak that repugnant language,' snapped Yelena. 'Translate.'

'It is difficult to translate directly, mistress,' replied *Starshyna*. 'But the gist of it would be – *We hunger for danger, and will die for the Legion.*

'And it is not simple rhetoric, mistress. If you get into a battle with these men, they will never surrender. You would have to kill every last one of them.'

Yelena chuckled. 'So be it,' she said. 'If they are harboring the Daywalker, we shall grant their wishes. No longer will they hunger for danger, because we will deliver it to them. In terminal doses.'

Starshyna bowed his head in acceptance. 'As you

say, so shall it be, mistress.'

'Yes,' confirmed Yelena. 'Now go back to your vehicle and continue to follow us. And no more unnecessary stops.'

'Mistress.'

Starshyna left and went back to his men.

CHAPTER 4

Emily stared in wonder at the mountain range in front of her. She had seen mountains before. Or she thought she had. But now she looked upon the Alps, she realized she had actually only seen mere hills before.

Mont Blanc dominated the horizon, even though it was many miles away, its snow covered peak some fifteen thousand feet above sea level.

'Are we still in France?' she asked Merlin.

The wizard nodded.

'How far to your place? Is it across the border in Italy, or still here?'

Merlin smiled. 'I don't mean to be obtuse, but technically, it's both and neither.'

Emily frowned. 'So, it's on the border?'

'Yes and no,' continued Merlin. 'Why don't you wait until we get there. It's easier than explaining.'

Emily nodded.

'Come on,' said Merlin. 'If everyone has had a chance to stretch their legs, let's get back into the vehicle. The next bit may prove to be ... disturbing.'

The team reboarded the van. No one bothered to

ask why the wizard thought the next part of the trip would be disturbing. After all, sometimes, ignorance is bliss. Especially when it is folly to be wise.

For the first time since any of the team had known Merlin, he took the driver's seat.

'Umm,' started Tag. 'You sure you can drive this thing?'

Merlin shrugged. 'I hope so. I can drive a coach and horses, surely this can't be much different?'

The collective look of horror on the hunters' faces as they stared at the precipitous drop next to the winding mountain road was a sight to behold.

'Merlin has been driving since the automobile was first invented,' interjected the Prof. 'He is merely joshing you.'

The wizard put the RV in gear and trod down on the accelerator, taking off at double the speed Muller had been driving. The wall of rock on the left side of the van rocketed past at a frightening rate, and every now and then the tires would scrabble on the very edge of the cliff as the road was so narrow.

They proceeded up the mountain pass at pace while the Prof mumbled to himself, muttering strings of calculations under his breath. The rest of the team stared pale-faced and white-knuckled at the narrow ribbon of blacktop as it spooled past them.

Merlin skidded around a corner and then took a sideroad left. It was less road and more like a natural fissure in the cliff face, barely wide enough to fit the vehicle through.

Emily looked through the windshield and saw that the fissure narrowed swiftly to a dead end some one hundred yards away.

'Merlin,' she yelled.

'Trust me,' he answered calmy.

So, they did.

The sound of Muller's praying almost drowned out the sound of the tires squealing as Merlin dropped a gear and hit the gas.

There was a thunderous crash, and the air grew as thick as treacle. Lights exploded in a riot of color so bright as to occlude sight. The world spun, and the vehicle juddered and shuddered as if it was about to shake itself to pieces.

Emily struggled to stop herself from throwing up as her stomach roiled and her inner ear rebelled like she was seasick. She heard the men retching as they were obviously afflicted with similar symptoms.

Except for Merlin and the Prof.

Then all movement stopped. The flashes of light slowly dimmed and the sounds faded away.

Emily realized she had closed her eyes and, as she opened them, the vista around her was revealed.

They were still in the mountains. But there was no sign of the narrow juncture Merlin had sped down. Nor the solid rock cliff he had smashed into.

Instead, they were near the very peak of a mountain that towered over all that surrounded it. In the distance she could still see Mont Blanc, but it looked tiny. Half the height of the peak they were parked on. And although she knew that was obviously impossible, it patently wasn't, as her eyesight attested.

'Where are we?' she asked.

'Still in the Alps,' answered Merlin. 'There, you can see Mont Blanc.'

'But, how?'

'Magic,' said the Prof.

'Obviously,' countered Emily. 'But how? I mean, are we still on earth? In the same plane? Or is this some sort of parallel universe?'

The Prof scoffed. 'No. We are still on earth. Merely in a hidden spot. An open area, if you will. Look on it as a folded section of space-time. Here and there but also neither.'

'I don't get it,' countered Emily.

'Well, if you have a spare couple of centuries, I might be able to explain it to you.'

Emily raised an eyebrow. 'No, I'll take your word for it.'

'Come on,' interjected Merlin as he alighted. 'Follow me, all of you. Let's get ourselves settled in.'

Emily turned to see the magnificent sprawling chalet perched on the side of the peak.

'Behold, my mountain hideaway,' continued the wizard as he trudged through the snow towards the front door.

The rest of the team clambered out of the vehicle

and trod in his footsteps.

With a flourish, Merlin opened the door. 'Welcome.'

'I hope you got some of that French stew,' proclaimed Tag. 'I is still hungry.'

CHAPTER 5

Yelena and Igor waited for the sun to go down before they left their blacked-out SUV to do some reconnaissance.

The Farm was surprisingly un-military looking. There was a fence, but it was only six feet high and wasn't electrified. There were no guard towers. No infrared beams and no dogs.

Only the warning signs placed every twenty yards or so gave any hint that the boundary contained a military base of sorts.

In French and English, on a red background with a skull-and-crossbones motif above the writing – *Beware. Live fire area.*

And that was it.

'You will all stay here,' commanded Yelena, her girlish, summery-light voice belying her dreadful appearance and her psychotic demeanor. She stared at the Spetsnaz familiar and sneered. 'And it would behoove you to try harder to not display your obvious relief,' she snapped. 'Coward.'

Starshyna kept his expression blank. Firstly, because he knew he had hidden his feelings of relief well enough for them not to show. Secondly, because he knew he was no coward and finally, because only an insane person would argue against someone like Yelena.

Unless, of course, they were attempting to commit suicide-by-vampire.

'Your will, mistress,' was his only answer.

'Right. Igor, can you control your Grinder?'

'He is not my Grinder, Yelena,' snapped Igor. 'As well you know. But anyway, the answer is, maybe. They are difficult creatures. He should be manageable, and I have strapped his mouth shut so he won't be able to give us away with that incessant whimpering of his.'

'If he misbehaves, kill him,' instructed Yelena.

'The Blood King will be less than pleased,' noted Igor. 'Seekers only come around once every century or so.'

'Fine,' retorted Yelena. 'Don't kill him. But if he messes up, maybe I will kill you instead.'

Igor shrugged. 'I will do my best. Shall we proceed?'

Yelena didn't answer, instead she jumped over the fence and disappeared into the encroaching darkness.

Igor took a firm grasp of Iscat's lead and followed, literally dragging the Grinder by his neck.

***

Johnny Baker was an American born member of the legion and had been one for six years. He had fought and bled for the Legion. So now he was considered to be, *Français par le sang versé.* French by spilled blood.

He had recently attained the rank of *Caporal-chef.* Some of his childhood friends whom he still kept in touch with teased him about the rank. Calling him a corporal-cook.

He simply smiled and laughed at their heavy-handed humor. Because the designation, *Chef,* had nothing at all to do with cooking. In fact, it came from the Latin word for head, or Chief. And it was an old cavalry tradition. The same rank could also be referred to as *Brigadier-chef,* which Johnny quite liked. It sounded much higher up the food chain than it actually was.

He was at the farm for an eight-month course before he applied to be considered for the next rank up - *Maréchal des logis.* Basically, a Sergeant.

And like everything the Legion did, it was incredibly tough.

He had just finished a solid four hours at the range and was heading back to the armory to sign back in his FN-minimi light machine gun and single one-hundred round belt of 5.56mm ammo he had left over.

As he walked, he passed a group of twenty Legionnaires and their Caporal returning from a thirty-mile run. He noted with satisfaction the men looked tired but not exhausted. Quite a feat when you considered they were all in full battle gear including their FAMAS assault rifles, one hundred and fifty rounds of ammunition, food, water, med supplies and grenades.

It was a source of Legion pride that all exercises were carried out with live ammunition and full kit whenever possible. It was true that partly due to this tradition the Legion suffered more deaths in training than any other elite force. But the powers that be deemed the attrition rate acceptable. As did the soldiers themselves.

The sound of boots on the ground faded as Johnny got closer to the armory, passing by the empty parade ground and then behind the vacant classroom barracks.

Then something made him stop. A sixth sense built up from spending time in places like French Guiana and the Central African Republic. Terrible, close up wars made up of countless skirmishes, ambushes and landmines. Places where the climate and the jungle killed you as often as the bullets and blades of the enemy.

And where many had died, Johnny Baker had endured. Because he learned, never ignore that feeling. That sixth sense had saved his life on more than a dozen occasions.

So strong was the feeling, he took the belt of ammunition from its pouch, opened the breech of the Minimi, loaded and cocked it. Technically, loading a weapon while not on the range and without express orders, was a punishable offence. But his combat honed instincts told him to ignore the rules.

Johnny stood motionless; head cocked to one

side as he strained to hear something out of the ordinary. Get some idea of what had triggered his senses. The longer he stood, the more intense the feelings got. After almost a minute he was literally sweating. Waves of horror and revulsion washed over him in equal measure. Still, he heard nothing.

Then he smelled it.

A strange combination of odors. Rotten meat with a faint hint of something chemical. Johnny sniffed the air. Nail varnish remover, he thought to himself. Weird.

Then, from out of the shadows they came.

At first, *Caporal-chef* Johnny Baker thought he might very well be hallucinating. Two humanoid beings, massively muscled, over six feet tall with features straight out of some sort of hellacious nightmare.

And standing behind them, being led by a long lead attached to a collar around his neck, was another similar version of the repellent creatures. Except this one had been gimped out to the extreme. Leather muzzle, leather mittens, some sort of gag. Hands and feet hobbled together by lengths of stout rope.

'So, this is one of the famed members of the mighty legion,' said the one apparition in a voice that seemed more suited to a young kindergarten teacher than the demon that actually spoke.

Johnny took a deep breath and forced his brain to react. He either had to accept, or reject what he saw. But whatever, he knew he had to do something, because even as nonplussed as he was, he could feel the waves of power rolling off the creatures.

He raised his machine gun. 'On your knees,' he commanded. 'Now, or I will shoot.'

The female laughed. A light, effervescent giggle. 'Idiot,' she said. Then she turned to the male version of hell standing next to her. 'Igor,' she said. 'Kill him.'

Johnny didn't hesitate.

The Minimi spewed out hot lead at a rate of twenty rounds a second and Johnny chewed through the entire one hundred round belt in one go. Brass poured from the breech and the air was filled with dust as the rounds stitched a pattern of death in front of the Legionnaire.

As the dust cleared, Johnny saw that all three of the nightmares had moved. Not by much. Just by enough to avoid the hail of death he had unleashed. He frowned as he replayed the scenario in his head.

Sighting the target.

Pulling the trigger.

At no point had he seen them move.

Johnny chuckled to himself. 'Fast,' he said.

'Yes,' agreed the female. 'That didn't work out as you thought it would, did it?'

Johnny shook his head.

'Anything to say before you die?'

'Yeah,' said the *Caporal-chef*. 'You wierdo's are beyond doubt the ugliest things I have ever seen.'

'Also, the most powerful,' snapped Yelena.

Johnny laughed out loud. 'Sure, you haven't met our Commandant. He makes you look like a pussy cat. And anyway, being powerful but having to look like you, let's just say, it wasn't a good trade.'

Igor snapped forward and punched Johnny in the ribs. The blow threw him back over ten feet and the sound of his rib cage breaking was clearly visible.

Johnny chuckled softly as he grimaced in pain. 'You hit like a girl,' he said.

Igor stepped towards him and picked him up by his shirt front.

'For the Legion,' grunted Johnny. 'Until the last one.'

And he spat in Igor's face.

The vampire exposed his canines, lunged forward and tore his throat out.

But as he threw Johnny's body to the floor, the air around him turned to fire, as the twenty Legionnaires Johnny had seen earlier, opened fire.

Igor was fast, and tough, and he healed at a rate that beggared belief. But in the next two seconds he was struck by over four hundred rounds of accurate fire. And it is impossible to heal parts of the body that no longer exist.

For example, his head exploded into a fine red mist, which left him rather cranially challenged, to say the least. His limbs were torn off and his torso was so full of holes you would have been able to see daylight through it. Had it not been night.

Then they turned their attention to Yelena.

But in that tiny period of time, Yelena had managed to tear off Iscat's restraints and, with a mighty heave, she threw the Grinder into the middle of the group of Legionnaires.

With a midnight screech, loud enough to rupture an eardrum, Iscat went apoplectic. Tearing and biting and punching. Like a wolf in a henhouse, he ripped through the soldiers, killing and feeding at the same time.

The Legionnaires fought back hard, but they were too close together to use their rifles or sidearms, so they had to go to blades and unarmed combat techniques.

But tough as they were, they were no match for a rabid Chernobyl enhanced Grinder. One by one they fell. Yelena stood to one side, ready to dispatch anyone who attempted to escape. But none did.

Finally, when there were three Legionnaires left, one of them ripped a grenade from his webbing, pulled the pin and, as Iscat turned towards him, thrust the live ordnance into the Grinder's mouth.

The resulting explosion killed the three soldiers and reduced the top half of the Grinder to ground meat.

Yelena swore. This was inconceivable. Two top combatants taken out by a group of mere humans.

And still they had not found where the Daywalker was, or what she was even doing here. She had to decide whether to continue her search or call it a night and beat a tactical withdrawal. But before she could, she heard someone approach.

'Now that must be the most hideous thing I have ever seen,' the newcomer announced.

Yelena turned to stare at him. He was of average height. Crewcut hair. Dapper moustache and some sort of rank flashes on his shoulder. He carried a M32 semiauto grenade launcher. A squad support weapon that allowed a single combatant to fire six, 40mm grenades as fast as they could pull the trigger.

Unfortunately, to kill someone like Yelena, you would have to hit them with at least two or three grenades. And to hit them, your reaction speed would have to be superhuman.

So, the vampire immediately dismissed the soldier as a threat.

'And who would you be?' she asked.

'Oh, it talks,' noted the soldier, raising an eyebrow in surprise. 'I am Commandant Quinton Swanepoel. And you?'

'Irrelevant. However, answer me some questions and I will kill you swiftly. Refuse, and your death will take forever. Where is the Daywalker?'

'Who?'

'I know she is here,' continued Yelena. 'Our Seeker tracked her down. She would have arrived with a small retinue including two old men and two or three younger ones.'

The Commandant looked genuinely puzzled. 'This is a military base. There are no civilians here.

It's forbidden. Man, are you stupid as well as ugly?'

Yelena concentrated, then she unleashed the full force of her coercion. 'Tell me the truth.'

Swanepoel flinched, but the vampire was surprised to see that he almost, but not quite, managed to shrug the coercion off. 'Hey,' he replied. 'I'm the Commandant here. I know who comes and who leaves, and this Daywalker person is not in this camp.'

Yelena knew the soldier was telling her the truth and she threw her head back and screeched with frustration. Not only had she been led on a wild goose chase, but she had lost her Seeker and her second. The Blood King would be furious.

Well, she thought to herself. At least I can feed off this idiot.

She moved.

At the same time, Commandant Swanepoel pulled trigger of his M32 as fast as he could.

Yelena ran straight into a maelstrom of explosions. Because Swanepoel had already seen how fast the vampires were. So, he made no attempt to aim at her. Instead, he aimed where he thought she would be.

And he got it exactly right.

The six high explosive grenades tore Yelena to shreds.

Swanepoel looked down at the tatters of flesh the grenades had reduced the vampire to. Then he took out a small cheroot, lit it, took a drag.

'For the regiment,' he said. 'Until the last one.'

CHAPTER 6

Tag placed a pot of tea on the kitchen table and passed out mugs to all. Then he turned to Merlin. 'I want to learn how to do magic,' he stated.

'No,' responded Merlin.

'Why?'

'Because.'

'That ain't no answer.'

'If I may,' interjected the Prof. 'I can teach you a little prestidigitation. That would be a start.'

'Predyi-who-what?' asked Tag.

'Prestidigitation. The art of small magics. Basically, practice spells for beginners. You know the sort of thing. Produce enough flame to light a pipe. Conjure a tiny gust of wind. Create a foul smell. Very minor spells. Then, once you have Mastered a few dozen of those, the real training can begin.'

'That's what I'm talking about,' grinned the big man. 'Let's start with fire.'

The Prof shook his head. 'No, no, no. It doesn't work like that. First you need to learn how to cycle your energies. Fill your cores and harness the power around you.'

'Cool. Let's do that then. How long will this take?

When can I light some stuff up?'

The Prof thought for a while. 'It all depends on you. But let's assume you have some inherent talent, and the will to learn. I would say … twenty years. Maybe more.'

'Twenty years,' exclaimed Tag. 'Before I can light a pipe.'

The Prof shook his head. 'No, you misunderstand.'

'Oh, thought so,' responded Tag with relief.

'Yes, it will be twenty years of study and inner contemplation and meditation before you can even *begin* to learn how to master the fire spell. That will take another three or four years. At best.'

'You serious?'

'Of course,' answered the Prof. 'Why do you think wizards and magical practitioners are so old? It takes many centuries to garner such skills. Sometimes thousands of years. So, shall we start?'

Merlin chuckled. 'There's little chance of that,' he said. 'Look, he's already lost interest. He hasn't got anything like the patience needed.'

Tag raised an eyebrow. 'I resent that comment,' he said loftily. 'I don't deny it, but I do resent it.'

Merlin laughed out loud. 'You have different strengths, big man. But I am glad you brought up the subject of training. Everyone, listen up.'

The team put down their mugs and paid attention. Except for the Prof who started mumbling to himself and sketching out random patterns in the air.

'Don't take this the wrong way,' stated Merlin. 'But in the year that I have been away, you lot have got slack.'

'Hey,' interjected Emily. 'We were taking a break.'

'Granted,' conceded the wizard. 'But a break is a couple of weeks. You basically slothed about for a whole year.'

'I wouldn't say we slothed about,' argued Troy. 'It's not like we lay around in bed all day and watched telly.'

'As good as,' said Merlin. 'How often did you train? Spar? Shoot? Work on your sword forms?'

Both Emily and Troy looked down.

'I thought so,' said Merlin.

'We didn't slack off,' stated Tag with a smirk.

'Yes, you did,' snapped Merlin. 'I know, the two of you continued to fight the good fight. But you got sloppy.'

'How would you know?' asked Muller. 'You weren't there.'

'Because, I know,' said Merlin. 'You cannot simply do what you do without a serious training regime. Okay, you stayed alive. Good. But as time goes on, your performance will degrade. Little by little. You are already not as sharp as you were when you trained every day. So, maybe not now, or even in six months, or a year, but sometime, those tiny, incremental losses of speed and form will kill you. Those uber-vamps you told me about...'

'The BUMF's,' interjected Tag.

'What?'

'Big Ugly Mother Fu...'

'Oh, yes,' said Merlin. 'Those. Ha, BUMF's good one. Anyway, they are obviously a cut above your usual bloodsucker. And if we start coming across them in numbers, well, they will kill you.'

'Hold on...' started Emily.

Troy butted in. 'No, Em,' he said softly. 'Merlin is right. I know you took out that BUMF relatively easily, but I struggled with mine. That's why I got so pissed when Muller helped. I wasn't sure if I could take him, and that scared me. I wanted to prove to myself I could do it.'

Emily frowned. 'If we're all being honest,' she admitted. 'I didn't find it as easy as you say. I had to go full out to take him down. He was fast, strong, tough and he healed faster than anything we have ever come across.'

'And ugly,' added Tag with a shudder. 'So ugly.'

Emily laughed quietly. 'Yes. True. But not sure if that made any difference to the actual fight.'

'So, what are you saying?' asked Muller. 'That we put together some sort of daily training routine?'

'Partly, yes,' answered Merlin. 'But *you* will not be putting the routine together.'

'Who then? You?' asked the Knight.

Merlin stood up. 'Come with me,' he said as he headed for the door.

The team followed the wizard outside and into the snow. The weather had worsened since they had arrived, and now an icy wind cut across the mountain, driving flurries of sleet and snow before it.

A few yards away, partially obscured by the eddies of snow, stood a man. He wore high top leather boots like a cavalry officer. Lightweight linen trousers and a leather jerkin that left his arms bare, despite the driving wind. His only nod to the weather was a full, brown woolen cloak that billowed about him. In his right hand he held a six-foot wooden staff with steel caps at both ends.

As the team walked closer, Emily noticed with a shock that she had been mistaken when she assumed the figure was human. Now that she could see him more clearly, his furred face, whiskers, and covering of light tawny fur, plus his obvious tail, belied his initial human appearance.

She pushed her senses out, attempting to get some sort of read off the figure. An idea of what he actually was.

But it was like she was concentrating on a rock. He gave off no discernable aura. Not even a noticeable sign of life. It was as if she were looking at a statue. Not a living being.

'People,' said Merlin. 'May I introduce the Fae weapons and combat expert, Master Ben Chu.'

Ben bowed slightly and walked forward. Emily noticed straight away that he left no footprints in the snow.

'Salutations, hunters,' he greeted. His voice was low and calm. Comforting, with a background purr to it, like a satisfied tabby cat. But his eyes were the eyes of a leopard, contradicting the gentleness of his speech.

Emily felt the werewolf part of her struggle to come to the fore as it perceived a rival alpha. She glanced sideways and saw that Troy was reacting the same way, his teeth elongating, his features changing. Not a full change, simply a showing of force. A statement.

I see you, and I show you my power.

It was a primal thing over which neither of them had full control.

Ben smiled at them, his canines glinting in the weak sun. 'Settle down,' he advised. 'Not here to challenge anyone. However,' he continued, and he spun his staff at such speed it became a mere blur. And such was the power he imparted, it literally tore a clear patch around him, blasting the wind-whipped snow away like he controlled his own personal tornado.

But at the same time, he projected an aura of calm. Relaxation.

Both Emily and Troy felt their inner wolves relax as the Master provided a tranquil balm to their senses.

'Wow, cool stick work, leopard-man,' said Tag.

Ben's demeanor changed instantly, and the feeling of calm was replaced by a maelstrom of anger. 'What you call me?' he growled.

Merlin stepped forward. 'Tag, calling one of the Moorfolk an animal is a deadly insult.'

'Why?'

'Because, *human*, I am no animal. Now, apologize.'

'Why?'

'You insult me.'

Tag shook his head. 'No, I didn't. You were insulted. But that's your problem. If I were to insult you, you would know. You gonna throw your toys out the cot every time someone says something you consider an insult? Hell, I call Troy, wolfman all the time. Imagine he went ballistic every time I did that. But, if it's an apology you're looking for, I'm sorry you get pissed for so little. There, happy?'

The Master turned to Merlin and raised a quizzical eyebrow. 'Are they all like this?'

Merlin grinned and nodded. 'In their own ways, yes.'

Ben looked at Tag for a moment and then nodded. 'Fine. Apology accepted, fat man.'

Tag smiled. And then frowned. 'Fat? Me, fat? I'll have you know this is all solid muscle. Well, mostly. Okay, I might have let myself go a little. Probably all that French stew … but, fat? I don't think so.'

The big man was about to expand on his argument when he noticed no one was listening to him, as Ben introduced himself to each of the rest of the team in person. Shaking them by the hand and offering a small bow.

'I have invited Ben here so he can oversee your training,' explained Merlin. 'He is a Master in all forms of armed and unarmed combat. In the Fae realm, Ben Chu is considered to be the Master of

Masters. Trust me, we are extremely lucky and privileged to have him.'

'I'm sure you're good,' stated Troy. 'I mean, that staff work was very flashy. However, and I mean no disrespect here, we are all pretty bad assed ourselves. What makes you think ...'

Troy didn't finish his sentence. On account of the fact that he was sprawled out, on his back, in the snow. A trickle of blood ran down his left temple.

None of the team had seen the Master move. Not even Emily.

'Fast,' noted Muller.

'Yeah,' concurred Tag. 'But how strong is he?'

Ben held his staff out towards the big man. 'Here,' he said. 'Take it from me.'

Tag scowled. 'Really? Is this some sort of trick?'

'No trick. Simply grasp the end of my staff, and take it from me.'

Tag contemplated the Master for a few seconds, and then he leaned forward, grabbed the end of the staff with both hands, flexed his muscles, and pulled.

Ben did not move. Not an inch. Neither did the staff.

'Come on,' said Muller. 'Put your back into it, big man. I've seen you uproot full grown trees and you can't take a stick off this little man.'

There was a hint of movement and Muller joined Troy in the snow. Tag still hadn't been able to move the Master. But somehow, the Moorfolk Master had downed the Knight while continuing to deny his staff to Tag.

Emily cocked her head to one side and decided to take a different tack. Instead of attacking physically, she called on her massive powers of coercion and launched them at the Fae Weapons Master, commanding him to release the staff.

For the first time, the Master looked visibly shocked. Tag still couldn't remove the staff, but it did appear to move perhaps an inch or two in his direction.

Then the Fae Master simply disappeared.

And Emily joined Troy and Muller in the snow.

Tag raised his hands. 'Last man standing,' he crowed. 'Who da man?'

There was a blast of air. A flurry of snow...

And Troy turned his head to look at the big man who was now lying next to him.

Without bothering to stand, Troy took out a pack of cigarettes, extracted, lit up, and blew out a puff of smoke that was dragged away by the wind.

'Well,' he said. 'Don't we look stupid.'

'A lesson in humility,' noted Muller.

'Yep,' agreed Emily. 'That didn't quite turn out like I expected.'

'I'm not fat,' said Tag. 'I'm burly.'

CHAPTER 7

'It entirely about control,' said the Master.

Emily shook her head. 'It's all a bit Karate Kid, don't you think?'

'I no idea what you talking about,' responded Ben. 'I know not of this young karate goat you speak of.'

'Kid as in child,' explained Emily. 'Not as in young goat.'

Ben shook his head. 'I do not care. Get back on top of tree stump and take form I have shown you. Stalking Crane.'

Emily frowned, but she jumped back onto the four-foot-high stump and assumed the position. Hands to her side, one leg up, supporting leg slightly bent.

The raw wind whipped at her loose top and thin linen trousers. She was absolutely freezing, but the Master insisted all wore no more than lightweight moccasins, and a thin linen tunic and trousers.

Cold was all in the mind, he said.

Emily wasn't convinced. It seemed as though the cold was actually in her bones. But after the display of skills Ben had shown the team, she was more than willing to follow his instructions to the letter.

And his first observation was – the entire team lacked control.

Mental, physical and spiritual.

Although he did admit that each of them was afflicted in varying ways.

For example, Muller had adequate spiritual and mental control, but he had fallen behind in his physical. Perhaps because he had been relying too heavily on Tag's strength and ability to stay alive.

Emily was physically acceptable, and her mental powers were off the charts. But she lacked control in every aspect of her being. She was badly out of balance and Ben was pleased Merlin had called him. Much longer and the Master doubted he would have been able to correct Emily's frightening tendency to allow herself to be steered towards the darkness.

Even now, he was not sure how much he could actually achieve.

Troy was an odd mixture. His physical control was good, and his spiritual aspect was strong. Most likely because of his bond with the Pack. Wolves are after all, very spiritual creatures. But anger and passion controlled him to a greater extent than they should. It was an inequality of emotions.

And then there was Tag.

The Master sighed to himself. If perfect imbalance was possible, the big man had achieved it. But that in itself made no sense. Because perfect imbalance was actually the same as perfect balance. To be honest, Ben was baffled. For the first time ever.

He decided that Tag was Tag, and all he could do for him was to make an attempt to steer him in the right direction and hope for the best. Because, when it came right down to it, Tag put all of his friend's lives above his own. His bluster and forthrightness covered a heart of gold and a capacity to sacrifice himself without thought or qualm.

In many other ways, he was a toddler in a giant's body.

Ben liked the big man very much. But he would never tell him that, he was already impossible enough.

He looked up at Emily as she balanced on the stump. 'Very good. Now, hold that for next two hours.'

'Two hours? Are you serious?'

'Yes,' answered Ben. 'This about control. After that, swop legs and hold for another two. Tomorrow, we try three.' The Master glanced at the wan sun. 'I see you in four hours. I need instruct the rest of the team.'

'I'll freeze to death in four hours,' snapped Emily.

'Try not to,' advised Ben. 'It would be inconvenient.'

And in the blink of an eye, he was gone.

Emily swore under her breath, but she continued to hold her pose, determined to do as she was instructed. She knew that, however strange

Ben Chu's instructions may appear, he was a Master in the arts, and his display of marshal power had been extremely impressive.

She started a mental countdown and tried her best to ignore the icy cold.

CHAPTER 8

The staff struck Troy again. Hard. Leaving a welt across his back. It healed almost instantly but it still hurt.

He moved fast, dropping below the next blow. But although he was fast, the Master was faster, and the steel cap on the end of the staff cracked against his temple.

Without conscious thought Troy began to change, allowing his anger to drive the process.

'Stop,' roared Ben. 'Balance. The wolf not control you. You not control wolf. Together, you are one. A perfect blend. Controlled existence. Balance.'

Troy forced the wolf down. And the staff smacked him in the head again.

'No. Do not seek subjugate the wolf. I not repeat myself; the wolf is you and you are the wolf. Tell me, Omega, how this so difficult for you? You not two separate beings, until you embrace that concept, you be a less efficient warrior.'

For the first time, Troy-wolf began to grasp what the Master was telling him. But it was not easy. The pack way had always been about dominance. Alphas, Omegas, leaders, followers. The wolf must be controlled. The human side was boss.

Now he saw how much energy that consumed. How inefficient it was. If both human and wolf could live in perfect harmony – then all of that wasted energy could go towards his ability.

More strength.

More speed.

More…

Ben Chu smiled. 'You begin see.'

And he hit Troy on the head again.

CHAPTER 9

Muller kissed his silver crucifix and tucked it into his linen shirt. He had been standing in the driving snow for over three hours now. Even though he had no watch, he knew how long it had been. This was because he had just finished reciting another fifty-three Hail Mary's, six Our Father's, five Glory Be's and seven other intercessory prayers. This ritual usually took him twenty-two minutes and he had just completed his eighth cycle.

Muller the Pious.

Waiting for the Master.

'Does that help?' asked Ben as he literally appeared next to the Knight.

To give Muller credit, he didn't jump, although if one had been looking closely, they would have noticed a slight tension around his eyes.

'Of course,' he answered. 'My God is everything.'

Ben nodded. 'I always found the gods to be capricious and, on whole, rather small minded.'

Muller smiled. 'There was a time when I would have condemned what you just said as blasphemy.'

'And now?'

'And now, I have met other gods. And some are

as you describe. Others, not so much. But one must always remember, my God is spelled with a capital "G".'

'So, He Omega of pack?'

Muller shook his head. 'He is the Alpha and the Omega. The First and the Last. The Beginning and the End. The One Who Is and Was and is Still to Come.'

Ben nodded. 'And you strive be like him?'

Muller chuckled. 'No, Master Ben, I strive to serve him. No more, no less. And I shall continue to do so to the best of my ability until death.'

'And I shall help you,' stated the Master. Using his staff, he scraped away a patch of snow to reveal a large boulder. It most likely weighed in at around six hundred pounds. 'Pick that up,' he instructed. Then he pointed with his staff to a tree standing twenty feet away. 'And place there.'

Muller frowned. 'It is too heavy, Master. I will be unable to do it.'

'Try,' insisted Ben.

Muller rolled his shoulders, rubbed his hands together, wrapped his arms around the rock and took the strain.

It moved.

Barely.

Less than a single inch.

'Told you,' proclaimed the Knight.

'Good,' said Ben. 'Continue trying. When becomes too dark to see, make way back to dwelling. Then tomorrow, get here first light. Repeat until give you permission stop.'

Muller watched the Weapons Master walk off into the swirling snow.

Then he bent down and began his next attempt.

CHAPTER 10

Tag looked suspiciously at the contraption that Ben had cobbled together.

Basically, it was a long length of thin rope that ran from a stake to a tree about fifty yards away. The other end of the rope was attached to a spring driven trapdoor in the bottom of a wooden bucket.

The bucket was filled with smooth pebbles, each as large as a golf ball.

'Okay, what's this?' asked the big man.

Ben leaned forward and pulled the rope. The trapdoor sprang open, and a single pebble fell to the floor. From yanking the rope to the pebble hitting the snow, it took perhaps two seconds. Maybe two and a half.

'It's a stone fall down bucket contraption,' noted Tag. 'So what?'

'Speed,' answered the Master. 'That what you lack. You have strength and healing, no speed.'

'Hey, I'm plenty fast,' argued Tag.

Ben shook his head. 'You slow, like pregnant hippo. Rely wholly on strength and invulnerability when fight.'

'And missus Jones,' added the big man.

Ben frowned. 'Once again,' he noted. 'You speak words make individual sense, but as whole they mean nothing to me.'

'Whatever,' responded Tag. 'So, what do you want me to do with the bucket thing?'

'Is simple,' answered Ben. 'I want you catch pebble.'

'Easy,' scoffed Tag as he strolled towards the bucket. 'Wait a second, then pull the rope when I'm ready.'

'Stop,' commanded the weapons Master. 'You misunderstand. Again. *You* need pull the rope.'

Tag frowned. 'Then how am I supposed to catch the stone? It's too far away.'

'Speed,' repeated the Master.

Tag looked at the rope. Then the bucket. Then the tree. And he laughed. 'What? Run fifty yards through the snow in two seconds?'

'Yes.'

'It's impossible.'

'For pregnant hippo. Yes. For vampire killing, superhero. Maybe not.'

'Am I the superhero?' asked the big man.

'Not yet.'

Tag nodded. 'Okay. I'll try. How many times?'

'Bucket full of pebbles. Try until bucket empty. Then fill bucket start again. When dark, come home.'

Tag sighed and walked towards the stake holding the rope.

'Wait,' said Ben. 'While you train, want you contemplate something. Because speed not just about physical. It also about mental. Speed will come as long as mind not thinking of it.'

'Seriously?'

'Yes. Seriously. Now, while you train, think on this. Nothing always as seems.'

'I don't get it. Like what?'

'Ben smiled. 'Like - how is it that sometimes, feet can smell and a nose can run?'

And the Master disappeared.

Tag stared at the empty space where Ben had just been. 'Crazy man,' he muttered to himself. 'Just friggin crazy.'

He leaned down and pulled the rope.

CHAPTER 11

Of all the amazing things that the humans had achieved, Arend considered the internet to be its acme.

Alas, to so many of them it was mere access to social media, or pornography. Few seemed to realize it as what it truly was.

It was the modern version of the lost Library of Alexandria.

Quite literally the font of all knowledge.

Okay, Arend was no fool. He did not allow the power of technology to pull the proverbial wool over his eyes. He could see that over ninety nine percent of all online content was absolute dross. But it was the one percent that was pure gold.

However, Arend was an arcane mage foremost and an ancient scholar second. His computer skills were close to non-existent. But after speaking to Hadad, he was put in contact with two other members of the team that were searching for the *Triginta*.

The identical twins, Monique and Mandrake DaCosta, cyber-info experts.

After communicating with them via a human

techno-miracle called Zoom or Skype or Grinder - to be honest, Arend couldn't recall - they had followed his leads, and within days come back with actionable intelligence.

The twins had hacked into a raft of websites, including government tax records, birth and death records, and banks as well as various privately run companies that looked into people's ancestry for a fee.

Compiling all of the available data, they had produced a list of progenies and a set of family genealogies relevant to the people who had most likely buried the body of King Euric.

Arend had cross referenced these names with the information he had, and voila – he hit a perfect match.

The information led directly to a German family, the Hoffmans, who lived on the isolated island of Hoffmanland in the North Sea off the coast of Germany. There were reputed to be barely a thousand people living there. However, although visitors were unwelcomed to the privately owned island, it was rumored that the Hoffmans were actually the leaders of a powerful cult.

A sect that worshipped the Hoffman's as gods and had to pay a substantial amount to the family in order to move to the island.

The family themselves ran a large hedge fund with their supplicant's money, and they had turned it into a staggering amount of wealth.

Arend could see the obvious signs of the powers

imparted by the *Triginta*.

And he knew he, and his colleagues, Mist and Remer, had to proceed to Hoffmanland Island as soon as possible.

He would charter a private jet.

The thought of Mist and Remer trapped inside a large steel flying box made Arend chuckle with anticipation. Another way to prove his sophisticated superiority over the noobs.

He called out to them.

'Mist, Remer. Ready yourselves, tomorrow morning early, we travel.'

CHAPTER 12

The boat transporting them to Hoffmanland ground up against the shoreline.

Half an hour at sea, standing on the deck and surrounded by water had helped Mist and Remer to recover from their nightmare in the metal flying box that had brought them to Germany.

Disappointingly for Arend, the flight had not affected the two *Hulder* as much as he had hoped. Obviously, they were already adjusting to the human world. On the bright side, they would be able to help him in a more efficient manner. He would just have to find some other way to amuse himself.

'Wait here,' he instructed the boatman. 'I will contact you when we are on our way back. We may be a few hours.'

The man gave the *Hulder* a quick salute and sat back in his chair, relaxing.

The team jumped onto the beach and ran into the forest that covered much of the island. The pine trees were loaded with snow, and they could see smoke rising in the distance from multiple chimneys.

'Right, the information the twins furnished us with show the cult leader's dwelling is on the north side of the island. He keeps himself detached from the general population. As the images they gave us showed, he is protected. High walls, dogs and a couple of guards. But I feel there is little to worry us. After all, he is not a high value target to anyone and this island is so isolated they do not expect anyone to break in.

'Once we are in, we find Herr Hoffman and question him as to the whereabouts of the *Triginta*.

'Then we relieve him of it, take our leave and get the boat back to the mainland. Any questions?'

'Do we kill Hoffman?' asked Remer.

'Only if we have to,' answered Arend. 'We shall incapacitate him, but no need to kill.'

Both Remer and Mist pouted. They were looking forward to a bit of wet work.

'Fear not,' Arend assured them. 'Before this quest is finished, I am sure there will be many chances to satiate your blood lusts.'

The three *Hulder* ghosted through the forest, as light footed and agile as they were rumored to be. The sun had risen about two hours before and as they ran, their acute hearing could pick up the sounds of the general population starting their days. The noises were unlike those of the current modern world, as the Hoffmans banned the use of motor vehicles on the island. Except, of course, for immediate family members. With them, no luxury was spared.

Solar and wind power provided the bulk of the electricity and the only way off the island was via sailboat. Or the Hoffman's fleet of luxury motor yachts, or private helicopters.

It was an island where everyone was equal. It was just that, some people were more equal than others.

The boundary wall to chief Hoffman's mansion loomed up out of the forest. It was around ten feet tall. No razorwire. A simple up and over job.

So, the three *Hulder* did just that, launching themselves over the wall with a little effort and a magical boost to their power, provided by a small spell from Arend.

A pair of Dobermans came dashing around the corner of the house, lips pulled back, snarling and frothing at the mouth.

The three *Hulder* looked at the animals with utter contempt.

Mist mumbled an arcane phrase and flicked a ball of lightning at them. There was a crackle of electricity and both canines fell, twitching to the floor, their fur smoking and steam rising from their burst eyeballs.

'Bit harsh,' noted Arend.

'Why?' asked Mist.

Arend shrugged. 'Actually, not sure why I thought that. Probably been with the humans for too long. You know, they keep them as pets.'

'What, like we keep pixies?'

'The same.'

Mist frowned. 'How very odd. Who would want a beast like that in one's dwelling?'

'They're very affectionate,' explained Arend. 'Sometimes they lick your face.'

Mist shuddered. 'Is that what those two were going to do?'

'No,' admitted Arend. 'Most likely they wanted to rip your face off.'

'Just as well then,' concluded Mist. 'Shall we continue?'

The three walked up to the front door. Arend tried the oversized door handle. It was locked. With a casual wave of his right hand, he blasted the lock out and they strolled in.

The entrance hall was a magnificent poem in marble and glass. A sweeping staircase curved upwards and the triple volume space above was dominated by a huge crystal chandelier.

Every possible surface that could be was leafed in pure gold.

Lifestyles of the rich and tasteless.

Remer nodded in appreciation. 'This human has good taste,' he noted.

As he spoke, a man in a dinner suit appeared from behind the staircase. Accompanying him was another man, this one in a lurid purple tracksuit and matching Nike trainers.

The man in the tracksuit was holding a pistol. With a sneer, he raised the weapon and pointed it at Arend.

'Just what the hell do you think you are doing;

you bunch of reprobates?' asked the man in the dinner suit.

Without pause, Remer cast a ball of fire at the gunman. About the size of a baseball, white hot and as fast as a National League pitcher, it struck the gunman's weapon, melted his arm off, incinerated the right-hand side of his torso and then went on to blast a hole through an awful portrait of some old person on a horse. Most likely one of the Hoffmans.

Purple tracksuit's corpse hit the floor with a squelch.

The dinner suit gasped and his attitude underwent a miraculous change.

'I am so sorry about the whole reprobate thing, sir,' he addressed Remer. 'How may I be of service?'

Remer giggled and chucked another fireball. It struck dinner suit in the face, causing it to explode in a cloud of red steam. 'Gosh, this is fun,' he crowed.

Arend smacked him on the back of the head. 'Idiot,' he snapped. 'I wanted to ask him some questions. You bloodthirsty fool.'

'He insulted us,' argued Remer.

'No,' responded Arend. 'He insulted me. You, however, are a reprobate. Now, for the sake of the gods, stop killing people until I've spoken to them. We need to find out where the head of the family is so we can get hold of the *Triginta*. Now, let me concentrate.'

Arend stood still, took a deep breath and then

released a spell. A wave of power swelled out like ripples from a pebble thrown into a lake. Ten seconds later, the wave flowed back. Arend nodded.

'Nineteen people in the house. Three upstairs, the rest towards the back of the dwelling. I think we can safely assume the owner is upstairs and the servants at the back. Let's go.'

He led the way up the stairs.

They reached the top of the stairs and Arend continued walking with a purpose. His two compatriots followed him down a corridor, through a couple of doorways and, finally, to a large set of double doors.

'They are in here,' he declared. 'Now, you can use a fireball. Blow the door down.'

Remer grinned and underhanded a fireball at the center of the double doors. It blew them both into the room like a burning tornado.

The sight that greeted the trio was ... let's say – unusual.

Arend noted three beings. A naked woman, tied to a chair, her face covered in what appeared to be honey.

A naked man, holding a riding crop, his flabby paunch hanging down over his private parts, with a pair of stout leather boots on his feet.

The third being was – well, Arend wasn't sure. It appeared to be some sort of reverse-centaur. A woman's body and a horse's head. She also had hooves for hands and feet.

Mist was the first to ascertain what the being

actually was. 'It's a mask,' she said. 'The woman is wearing a horse-head mask.'

Remer burst out laughing. 'My, aren't humans interesting,' he observed.

'What? How? Who are you?' shouted the naked man.

The woman on the chair stared lasciviously at the facsimiles the *Hulder* trio had donned, and she licked her lips. 'Yummy,' she said. 'I like.'

'Are you Hoffman?' asked Arend.

'Get out.'

'Can I kill him?' asked Remer.

'Shut up,' snapped Arend. 'Not yet. Now, I politely ask again, for the last time, are you Hoffman?'

The man took a few steps towards the Fae leader and swung his crop at his face. Arend didn't even bother to dodge. Instead, he simply flicked a tiny sphere of energy at the man's hand.

The crop stopped abruptly, as if the man had struck a wall, and then, with a pop like a bursting party balloon, his hand exploded.

'Do you see?' Arend said to Remer. 'Control. No need for massive balls of fire. And now, we can still question him.'

As he was lecturing his compatriot, the horse-masked woman slunk to the side of the room and used her plastic hoof to press a panic button. In the main village close to the house, alarm bells rang and people gathered.

Arend walked over to the naked man, who was

now kneeling in the floor holding his wrist and staring at the shattered remains of his hand. At the same time, he rocked back and forth, keening shrilly.

Arend spun a gag out of air and slammed it against the man's mouth to stop the noise. Then he used another air construct to bind the man's wound.

'Right,' he proclaimed. 'I will remove the gag in a few seconds. When I do, the first thing that comes out of your mouth will be the whereabouts of the *Triginta*. Understand?'

The man stared up at him, his eyes filled with a mix of fear and confusion.

'And, done,' said Arend as he dispelled the gag.

'I don't know what the *Triginta* is,' the man stammered.

'Blow his leg off,' yelled Remer.

Mist giggled.

Arend held up his hand. 'No. No. Fair enough. He probably has no idea what I'm talking about. My bad. Let me explain. A necklace or torc, made up of silver coins. Roman ones.'

Recognition flared in the man's eyes. But he shook his head. 'Sorry,' he whined. 'I still have no idea.'

Arend frowned. 'Now, you see, you are lying to me.'

'No, I swear.'

A flick of the fingers and the man's left foot exploded.

craig zerf

Another gag of air halted the screaming.

The trio of Fae watched the naked man thrash about on the floor in agony.

'Why won't he tell us?' asked Mist.

Arend shrugged. 'Not sure. Most likely he knows that the family's power stems from it. Maybe he's simply braver than I gave him credit. Tell you what, let's start with the horse faced lady. Chop a few limbs off. Maybe she knows.'

The women in question ripped her mask off to expose a shrew-like face. Pinched features, large, pointed nose and a massive squint in her left eye.

'Please,' she gasped. 'I'll tell you where it is.'

'And who are you?' asked Arend.

'I'm Leticia Hoffman.' She pointed at the man on the floor. 'That is Frank Hoffman. Leader of the congregation.' Then she pointed at the woman tied to the chair. 'She's a whore.'

'I'm not,' shouted the chair-woman. 'I'm a faithful follower.'

'Oh, shut up,' snapped Leticia.

'So, Frank is your husband?' assumed Arend.

'Brother,' corrected the horse woman.

A flicker of disgust rippled across Arend's features. 'You play...never mind. Disgusting. So, you can show us?'

'Yes. The artifact of which you talk is the family's most prized possession. We call it, the Cup of Power.'

'Why?'

'Because it's a cup,' explained Leticia. 'And it

gives us power.'

'I am looking for coins,' replied Arend.

Leticia nodded. 'Yes. There are three coins attached to the cup. Fixed to the side. Roman coins.'

'Where is it?'

'In the study. I will show you. Follow me.'

'Can I kill him now?' asked Remer, pointing at the fallen man.

'No,' replied Arend. 'Wait. Let us see if this creature is telling the truth.'

The naked horse-girl trotted out in front of them. She had removed her mask, but retained the plastic hooves on her hands and feet.

'Hey, what about me?' shouted chair girl.

Arend rolled his eyes. 'Mist. Take care of her.'

Mist turned back into the room. There was a sharp pop and the female *Hulder* returned, wiping a spot of blood from her cheek.

'All done.'

Arend stared at her. 'I meant untie her.' He shook his head. 'Never mind.'

Horse girl opened a door and gestured for them to follow. They entered a study. Large, well appointed. More gold leaf.

Then horse girl grasped the frame of a huge painting situated over the desk. It was a glamorized version of the naked, paunchy man from the bedroom. In the painting he was more Napoleon and less Sad Sack.

With a grunt of effort, she pushed the painting to one side, running it silently on a set of tracks to reveal a safe door. Then she placed her hand on a screen next to the safe. Locks spun and the door clicked open.

Arend nudged her to one side and peered in. There were stacks of shrink-wrapped currencies of various types. A few jewelry boxes. A small statuette of a horse.

And a silver goblet.

Arend snatched the goblet up and studied it. Even before he noted the three coins soldered to the sides of the artifact, he felt the power. It throbbed in his hands like it had a heartbeat.

Visions of control and influence wielded came to him. Arend in charge of thousands. King. President. Anything he wanted. Loved by all. Worshipped by many.

But he was not swayed by them. Because all that drove Arend was his thirst for knowledge. And the prize he had his eyes on was more important than anything the *Triginta* could offer him.

With a sigh of relief, he stowed the artifact in his jacket pocket.

'Is that it?' asked Remer.

'Yes. Now we have six of the thirty.'

'Can I kill the naked man?'

Arend nodded. 'If you want. Be quick.'

'What about me?' asked horse girl.

'Oh, of course. You,' responded Arend. 'Remer, you can kill this one as well.'

'No,' screamed Leticia.

'Yes,' chuckled Remer.

Pop.

Arend strolled from the room and headed for the stairs.

Behind him he heard Remer laughing loudly as he exploded Frank Hoffman.

Mist walked beside him.

As they reached the bottom of the stairs, Remer caught up. He was rubbing his hands together in glee.

'Haven't had so much fun since the Goblin insurrection,' he said.

Arend opened the front door to exit the mansion.

To be confronted with a huge mob of people. They were carrying various weapons. Shotguns, swords, poles and axes.

'What have you done to mister Hoffman?' shouted one of them.

'What the hell?' grunted Arend in surprise.

'Happy days,' crowed Remer. 'Can I kill them all?'

CHAPTER 13

Arend shook his head in exasperation. Why was everything so darned difficult?

'Fine,' he said with a heavy sigh. 'Have fun, both of you. You deserve it.'

Remer wound up a spell, but just before he managed to release it, one of the mob members fired his shotgun at the *Hulder* combat mage.

Instinctively, Remer threw up a hasty shield and most of the buckshot was diverted. Although a couple of pellets punched through and struck him in his right shoulder. Remer looked at the wound in amazement.

'Hey, that peasant just attacked me with a thunder-stick.'

'Stop that right now,' snapped Arend. 'Remember when I warned you two about using stupid, dorky, noob language?'

Both Mist and Remer nodded.

'Well, *thunder-stick* most definitely falls into that category. It's a shotgun, you moron.'

Another shotgun boomed out. But by now, Arend had erected a full shield and the buckshot ricocheted harmlessly off it.

'Just so we don't offend again,' interjected Mist, ignoring the screaming mob as being rather inconsequential. 'What exactly does *dorky* mean?'

'And *noob*,' added Remer.

'Whatever,' sighed Arend. 'Just get rid of the peons so we can leave.'

Remer whooped and started throwing fireballs around like he was giving away free samples.

Mist preferred mini-tornados.

Both were equally effective.

As in, not very.

The problem was, they were taking the mob out piecemeal.

The fireballs would punch through someone and then explode, usually putting them down, sometimes simply maiming them.

Mist's mini-tornados were even less affective as an area attack. They would tear into a single person, smash them to the ground, and roll them about while ripping off their clothes and slowly, very slowly, shredding their skin and flesh.

Meanwhile, Arend had to enlarge his force shield in order to stop them being overwhelmed by the mob.

He was about to express his utter distain towards his compatriots' feeble attack spells when he noticed the expressions on their faces. Or to be more correct, the expressions on the faces of the simulacrums they had adopted. But that was mere semantics, because the glamor's they had assumed, mimicked the actual wielder's expressions quite faithfully.

And that expression was one of absolute glee.

Arend had wrongly assumed the two of them were weak. Whereas, in reality, they were just enjoying themselves. Wringing out as much individual suffering on their targets as possible.

Cat and mouse.

With a chuckle, and a fatherly smile of, not quite pride, but at least slight approval, Arend kept up his force shield and allowed the noobs some fun.

However, after twenty minutes he began to lose patience. More Hoffmanlanders were arriving and, quite frankly the wanton violence was starting to bore him.

'Right, that's enough,' he stated as he wound up a massive area effect spell. With a slight grunt of effort, he unleashed it. A wave of power crashed out, causing a semi-solid wall of air to speed outwards and crush everything in its path.

The windows in the mansion shattered, doors imploded, walls cracked and roof tiles flew off like a hurricane had struck.

The human mob disintegrated. A foul sleet made up of human flesh and innards and bones coated the snow, turning the pristine white winter-wonderland into a Hieronymus Bosch nightmare.

'And that is how you do it,' snapped Arend. 'Now, let's move. Places to go, artifacts to discover and quite possibly, more humans to kill.'

Both Remer and Mist pouted their displeasure at Arend taking their toys away.

70

But after the awesome display of power they had just witnessed, neither dared actually voice their displeasure.

CHAPTER 14

The table was over fifty feet long. Carved from the bones of the dead and lacquered in their blood. It was like a slab of red-black onyx. Torches flickered along the walls, creating more shadow than light.

Seated at the table, a mélange of various gods, godlings, banshees, demons and monsters.

At the head of the table sat, *Dhuosnsos*, often referred to as the Donn. The Celtic god of the dead. It was in his abode the meeting was taking place, although it was at the Morrigan's behest.

Standing to one side, in her form of a beautiful woman, stood the Morrigan. Her dress just wisps of blood red cloth as opposed to actual clothing. The cloth moved of its own accord as she paced back and forth, covering and revealing in equal measure.

Given her looks and her body, it should have been a spectacle of great desire. The epitome of carnal lust.

But the expression on her face ensured that any thoughts of desire were expunged from a viewer's mind. It was a look of such hatred, such rancor and malice, that it conjured little more than either fear, or grudging respect, depending on the entity who was presently observing.

'Humanity is weak,' ranted the Morrigan. 'They have forgotten the old gods. But no more. We must bring them back into the fold. By force if necessary. Because that is all they respect.

'They must be torn from their new false idols of technology and reality television.

'Punished.

'We must ferment war. Pestilence, to drive their worship, get them begging for a savior.

'Anarchy must be encouraged. And to start it all, we need to destroy anyone who stands against us. Particularly the Shadowhunters. The werewolves. Merlin.

'Let the vampires run free, let terror stalk the night until the only way for the humans to turn is towards us.'

There were murmurs of both agreement and dissent. Then the Donn talked. His voice rumbled across the room, like an avalanche of rocks. A force that carried with it more than mere sound. It was power incarnate. The power of forever. Of the end of all things.

The power of Death.

'Warrior woman,' he growled. 'This quest of yours smacks of a personal vendetta. And many of us, unlike yourself, do not necessarily thrive on war.'

'Personal? Yes, perhaps,' admitted the Morrigan. 'But is this not personal to all of us. Is it not our collective worship that wanes? Anyway – why shouldn't I get my revenge? Merlin imprisoned me. He cast me aside like a filthy rag. And all because of her. That girl and her friends. She must suffer. They must all suffer for what they did to me.

'Surely, you of all of the gods should approve. After all, wholesale destruction, war and pestilence will pack your halls many times over. Think of all the death. You will have your fill and more.'

'Cease your termagant ravings, harridan,' roared the Donn. 'You assume, because I am the Lord of darkness, the King of the dead, that I will support your infantile tantrum. You think that I will support death and anarchy?'

The Morrigan leered. 'As you said, you are the Lord of death. The prince of the dark. How can you not support my quest?'

The Donn shook his head. 'Darkness is not evil,' he said. 'It is merely the absence of light. Nighttime is not a time for evil to stalk, it is a time for rest. Sometimes, eternal rest.

'I am not saying I condemn evil. Far from it. Both are needed for proper balance. Evil provides mankind something to fight against. Humanity is sword-born, and by the sword shall they perish. They yearn for battle. The darkness gives them something to rail against. Yes – I am dark - But do not assume I am evil.

'And beware, - the old gods have had their time. Do not seek to fight against humanity, they are powerful beyond your comprehension. They are many. And every day there are more of them.'

'But we are powerful,' argued the Morrigan.

The Donn scoffed. 'Are we? Look closely at the journey you are about to embark on, war goddess. Be careful that you do not get what you look for. I am the only constant. Death. You are but a fleeting moment in time. Even war has an end.

'Now begone, foul woman. I am sure there are some who may support you, but I am not one.'

The Morrigan was so incensed she shimmered and almost shifted into her giant crow form as she came close to losing control. The only thing that kept her from attacking the Donn was the knowledge that the King of the dead was all powerful in his domain.

What he said was the Lore.

Taking a deep breath, she turned and left the hall, striding through the stone arches and into the vast open cavern that marked the entrance to the land of shadows.

She stood for a while; half hidden in the gloom. Alone.

Then she sensed a presence and turned to see the massive figure of Balor standing behind her.

The gigantic cyclops, leader of the Fomorians, a group of malevolent supernatural beings, nodded a greeting.

The Morrigan turned away, ignoring him.

'Do you recall the battle of *Mag Tuired*,' he asked.

Still the Morrigan did not react. Truth be told, she was wary. As the goddess of war, she was afraid of no one or nothing. But if she ever was to feel any fear, Balor might be the one to invoke it. He was a ruthless warrior, and his followers were denizens of evil.

Some call him the cyclops god, or the evil eye, others, the lord of destruction. He was a malicious and spiteful demi-god. Not to be trusted. But when you have little choice, sometimes one is forced to sleep with the enemy.

'I remember it well', replied the Morrigan. 'Arthur bested you.'

'No,' fumed the giant. 'Excalibur bested me. Curse that enchanted sword. Thanks to the gods of chaos, it is no more. And curse Arthur king, and his lacky, Merlin. I will stand with you, crow woman.'

The Morrigan thought before answering. But she knew, the enemy of my enemy is my friend – for now.

She spat on her palm and held it out. Balor did the same.

They clasped hands and shook once.

Oathbound.

The Morrigan smiled. It was a beginning.

CHAPTER 15

'Time moves differently in folded space,' said Merlin.

'How differently?' asked Emily. 'To my reckoning we've been here for over three months and I'm worried what is happening in the real world.'

Merlin chuckled. 'This is also the real world,' he said. 'It's just running parallel at the moment. But it is still a part of our universe.'

'How long?' asked Emily again.

'You are correct,' answered Merlin. 'We have been here just over three months in present time. But in the Real World, as you like to put it, it's been around three, maybe four days.'

Emily frowned. 'How is that possible?'

'It isn't,' quipped Merlin, and he wiggled his fingers at Emily. 'But somehow, I make it happen.'

Emily was about to question the wizard further, when Ben appeared in his usual fashion. One moment, no Ben, next instant, Ben.

'Training,' he said.

Emily shook her head. 'Don't want to. I've been standing on that tree stump every day, all day doing that stupid Crane Kick for three months now. I'm sick of it.'

Ben nodded. 'Fine. Follow me. Today we change things.'

He walked off into the snow and Emily followed. As they walked further from the house her ears picked up a sound of running water. Then a waterfall.

After another twenty minutes of fast walking, they exited the forest. In front of them stood a small waterfall. It was around thirty feet high and the water splashed down onto a rounded boulder below, throwing up an impressive amount of spray that became sleet as the frigid air cooled it to freezing point.

The Master pointed at a tree stump situated directly in the path of the majority of the frozen spray.

'There,' he said. 'Get on stump. Assume the position. Kick. Repeat until nightfall.'

'Hold on,' interjected Emily. 'That's exactly the same thing I've been doing for the last three months.'

Ben shook his head. 'No. Last three months no freezing waterfall. Assume position. Now.'

Emily scowled and then obeyed. She jumped onto the stump, assumed the Crane position and kicked. But the ice-covered wood was like greased glass and she flipped over and fell to the ground.

'Get up,' commanded Ben. 'Continue. I see you tonight.'

He disappeared.

Emily clambered back onto the tree stump, stood on one leg, kicked.

And fell again.

She swore under her breath. This was going to be a long day.

Ben watched her from a distance. What none of the students realized was that the Master didn't teleport away, he simply faded into the background. He was there, but they could not see him or detect him in any way. He had become one with his surrounds.

The girl worried him. Of all of the students, she was the most problematic. And by far the most powerful. Much more powerful than he was. Or possibly even Merlin.

But she had no balance.

That was what he was trying to rectify. Hence the constant repetition of the same movement, The Fighting Crane. And now he had added a further level of discomfort with the freezing spray and the ice-covered stump.

Because Ben Chu knew that through mindless repetition one could eventually achieve a form of enlightenment. When the body and the task became one, that was when the mind would open to the next step. The ability to accept oneself. Until Emily allowed herself to be happy with what she was, there would be no balance.

Presently, she hated part of her own soul. She despised the darkness in her. She railed against it.

Instead, she should be accepting it. Not allowing

it to rule, but accepting that it was a part of her.

For when she stopped fighting, then she would rob that part of her of any power. One cannot win a battle that is not being fought. That is what she had to understand.

But it would take a while longer. Her journey was long, and difficult, and it had barely begun.

Ben turned his back on her and made his way to see Muller.

***

The Knight of the Holy See concentrated on his task, rubbed his hands together, bent forward and clasped the boulder, wrapping his arms around it as much as he could. He took the strain and, achingly slowly, he stood up.

Then he walked. One staggering step at a time.

After ten steps he yelled out as his muscles began to quiver in exhaustion.

'Come on. Muller,' he cajoled himself.

Another step. And another.

Finally, with a cry of frustration, he dropped the massive rock and fell to his knees.

He had just walked a dozen steps, in the deep snow carrying a boulder weighing well over a thousand pounds.

A feat that was technically impossible for a human being to achieve.

Ben allowed himself to be seen.

'Master,' greeted the Knight.

'Muller. You have done well.'

'Thank you.'

'You know how to meditate?' asked the Master.

'I meditate through prayer.'

'Fine. Spend rest of the day doing so. Open mind. Accept all round you. Become one with it. Do until I give further instructions.'

'Yes, Master. Will that be later today?'

Ben raised an eyebrow. 'I will see you in few weeks. Remember, every day, out here in snow. Open your mind.'

He disappeared.

***

Troy sat cross legged on the ground. The drifting snow piled up on his shoulders, the top of his head and all around him to a depth of a couple of feet.

He did not move. His eyes were closed and the only sign of life was the occasional plume of vapor as he breathed out.

Ben brought his staff down hard.

But Troy blocked the blow with ease, throwing his right arm up and deflecting the staff past him.

He did not open his eyes.

He did not move.

Ben Chu smiled and vanished from sight.

***

The Master contemplated Tag with an expression that looked to be a combination of awe and confusion.

Three weeks before, Ben had set the big man

a task that was impossible to achieve. He had to catch a pebble falling from a tree over fifty yards away. To accomplish this goal, he would have to cover the ground, while wading through the snow, in under two seconds.

He had not been able to do so.

However, he was close. Mere inches away.

He had somehow managed to increase his speed to something approaching three times that of an Olympic sprinter.

The Master was thinking on how Tag had achieved this when he became aware of someone standing behind him. He turned to see the Prof.

'How you do that?' asked Ben.

'What?'

'Sneak up on me like that. Is not possible.'

'Obviously it is, old chap,' returned the Prof as he took out his pipe and lit it with a small conjured flame. 'And anyway, I wasn't sneaking, I was simply coming to see Tag. Remarkable specimen, isn't he?'

'Specimen?'

'Yes, you know, subject, specimen. Experiment, I suppose.'

'He not your friend?' asked Ben.

The Prof puffed his pipe and thought for a moment. 'Yes. I suppose he very well might be.' He looked surprised. 'Well, I never. Who would have thought?'

'He most definitely conundrum,' acknowledged Ben.

The Prof chuckled. 'Tag is more than that,' he said. 'He is an enigma, wrapped in a conundrum and placed inside a puzzle box. His biology and his mental makeup are quite extraordinary. You know, before I started experimenting on him, he was just a normal chap. Well, as normal as Tag could ever be. But now, super healing ability, super strength and, as far as I can make out, super speed.'

'How?'

The Prof shrugged. 'No idea. I have injected, and he has ingested so many different potions that I have lost track. Awful of me, I know, but sometimes I get overexcited.'

The two stood in silence for a while.

'I need ask a favor of you,' said Ben Chu.

'Fire away.'

'I want you teach Tag magic.'

The Prof laughed. 'Can't be done,' he said.

'Why?'

'The chap has the attention span of a squirrel.'

'Yet here he is, after three grueling weeks, still doing same thing. Improving every day,' pointed out Ben.

Again, they simply watched. Thinking.

'When I set Tag task,' said Ben. 'I also told him contemplate question. How can feet smell and noses run?'

The Prof chuckled again. 'Poor chap, there's obviously no answer to that. Why'd you do it?'

'To clear mind. I told him ponder question while he attempted task. Here my deal, if he able to answer question, you try to teach him?'

The Prof frowned. 'It is an unanswerable question. But, yes, if he could.'

Ben called out to the big man, beckoning for him to come over.

Tag jogged up. Hi, Master. Prof.'

The Prof nodded. 'Greetings ... friend.' He smiled.

'You done well, my pupil,' said Ben. 'Now, you considered question?'

'Yes, Master.'

'And what your answer?'

'Master, if your feet can smell and your nose can run – you are most probably hanging upside down.'

Nobody spoke for a few seconds.

Then the Prof laughed. 'Fine,' he said. 'I shall, teach him. Or at very least, I shall try.'

Ben bowed low,

And vanished.

CHAPTER 16

'I am a monster,' said Mikael Trotsky. 'And it is his fault.'

The hideously deformed vampire accepted a Cuban cigar from his host. He eschewed a cigar cutter and bit the end off instead. Then he produced his own Zippo and put the cigar to flame.

Kievan Romanoff did his best to look his guest in the eye and not shudder. After all, it would not behoove the head of House Romanoff to exhibit such crass emotions.

'In what way?' he asked Trotsky, genuinely curious as to why the monster hated Belikov so much.

'I was living with a small group of brethren in a village close to Vladivostok. I was happy. We hunted at night, entertained. The locals served us well. But then the Blood King called me. He wanted me to bring my clan and join him at his palace next to the Pipyat River. Just outside of Chernobyl.

'None of us wanted to go. But the Blood King is very powerful. And vindictive. So, we went.

'We arrived on April the 16th, 1986,' said Trotsky. 'Ten days later, Chernobyl had a meltdown.' He dragged heavily on his cigar. Then he gestured towards his own face. The mushroom-like growths, the rough flaps of wattled skin, the dark gray and livid purple ridges. 'I became what you now see before you.

'A grotesque. A side show freak. Something fit only to hide in the shadows like some deformed Hyena.

'He must pay. The Blood King must pay for what he did to me and my clan.'

Romanoff frowned. 'That is all well and good, comrade,' he said. 'But we are talking about the *Krov Tsar.* Even to whisper the words you are saying is a death penalty. True death.'

'He has his weaknesses,' insisted Trotsky. 'His arrogance, for one. He has no idea how much he relies on his second, Jebe Zurgadai. The man is meant to be his friend, but he treats him more as a pet. A dog to be patted on the head when he begs for a treat.

'Also, he cannot comprehend that anyone would turn against him. His conceit is so large he considers himself untouchable. We can exploit that. All we need is to remove Jebe from the picture for a short while. Or permanently, I don't care. I am personal friends with a number of Belikov's guards, trust me, there is no love lost there. I will ensure they are looking the other way, then we strike. Behead the Blood King and offer his body to the rising sun.'

'Yes, I see,' remarked Romanoff. 'But where does house Romanoff fit into this audacious plan of yours?'

'I will need backup,' answered Trotsky. 'House Belikov is divided. The Blood King rules through intimidation and fear.'

'Don't we all?' interjected Romanoff.

'Yes, of course,' conceded Trotsky. 'But the better leaders temper that with respect. The brethren will always follow a Master that engenders both fear *and* respect. Belikov is all fear.

'But to fully answer your question, I need a team of your best warriors. Masters, or Ancients at least. Because you must not forget, although we at house Belikov have been cursed with repulsiveness, we have also been blessed with great physical speed and strength.

'Give me twenty of your best. And then have the rest of your people waiting for my call. As soon as we have destroyed the Blood King, you will swoop in and validate my rule over house Belikov.

'It will become, house Trotsky.'

'What is in it for me?' asked Romanoff.

'We would have a formal agreement as allies,' answered Trotsky. 'Also, we would get rid of the Blood King who seeks to join all *Nosferatu* under his banner. We both know that is an unnatural existence for our kind. It will never work.'

'Yet you propose an alliance,' argued Romanoff.

'That is different. The brethren have often had loose alliances. As long as it benefits both houses, it is acceptable. But to kowtow to a single ruler.' Trotsky shook his monstrous head. 'No. I spit on the Blood King and his aspirations.'

'Let me think on your proposal,' countered Romanoff. 'I shall take council with my people and get back to you. Meanwhile, please treat my house as your own. We have a new batch of food, teenagers fresh from the Ukraine. Help yourself.'

Trotsky stood. 'I give thanks,' he said as he left the room.

CHAPTER 17

Kick. Switch legs. Jump. Kick. Repeat. A hundred, a thousand, ten thousand times.

The ice crackled on Emily's thin linen shirt and pants. The wind whipped her ponytail from side to side and the snow swirled around her like a crystal dust storm.

Kick.

Kick.

Every movement was perfect. Even though the tree stump was coated in ice, her feet did not slip.

The sun rose.

The sun set.

She had been doing the exact something for twelve hours a day, seven days a week, for six weeks.

Breath in.

Breath out.

Every kick expelled a little more of her anger. Her frustration. And slowly, incrementally, the level of rage in her system lessened.

And on the afternoon of the forty-second day - Emily stopped.

And she smiled.

She jumped down from the stump and began to walk back to the house.

'I can see you,' she said.

Ben Chu chuckled. 'That is pleasing. And unusual. Why have you stopped? The sun has at least three more hours before it retires.'

'I have finished doing that,' answered Emily.

'What have you finished doing?' asked the Master.

'Fighting nothing. Fighting everything. I have finished standing on an icy tree stump in the snow and kicking at emptiness.'

'Why?'

'Because I have come to a realization,' answered Emily.

'And what is that?'

Emily stopped walking and turned to face the Master. 'I have come to realize that for the past ten weeks, I have been fighting myself.'

Ben smiled. Then he bowed. 'Well done, student,' he said. 'Go back to the abode. Eat. Rest. We shall talk again tomorrow.'

CHAPTER 18

Another six months passed in folded space. All in all, the team of hunters had spent just over a month in Real World time.

The last couple of folded space months, Ben Chu had drilled them in their basics. Kata, swordplay, unarmed combat, archery and firearms. Even some explosives work.

As well as these skills he continued to coach each member in the areas he felt they needed most work.

There was no doubt that the four of them were now in the best shape they had ever been. Both mentally and physically.

Tag was also the most frustrated he had ever been.

The Prof had taken him for four hours every day and tutored him in the skills of basic magic.

Meditation, concentration and contemplation.

'Enough *Om Mani Padme Hum*,' Tag said loudly. 'I wanna get to the *Flame On* part of this stuff.'

The Prof looked puzzled. 'What you are doing has nothing in common with the Sanskrit mantra associated with the four-armed Shadakshari form of Avalokiteshvara, the bodhisattva of compassion,' he said. 'The exercises I am teaching you are all to do with concentration of power, not the realization of empathy.'

Tag frowned. 'Sure, Prof,' he acknowledged. 'I have no idea what most of the words in that sentence meant. All I'm saying is, how much longer do I have to keep doing this meditation before I can burn stuff?'

'Forever,' answered the Prof. 'It must become a daily habit. You need to surpass the first level in order to be able to draw upon the latent power of the universe. Until then, no *Flame On*. Not even *Small Spark On*. Continue, big man. But do not feel discouraged, already you are further down the path than you think.'

The rest of the team grinned at Tag's discomfort.

'Listen up, people,' interjected Merlin. 'It's been a month out there, and it's time to get back in the saddle. I've collected some info and have a couple of *Nosferatu* Houses we need to strike. Gather round the table and I will lay it all out for you.'

'What about me?' asked Tag. 'I can't even light a cigarette with my magic.'

'Yeah, but you can burn a house down with Missus Jones,' offered Troy.

Tag smiled. 'That be true and all, but truth be told, I'm looking to do things in a more cereal way from now on.'

'Cereal?' asked Emily.

'Sure, you know, using your brain instead of

your brawn.'

'Oh, cerebral.'

'That's what I said.'

'Tag,' said Merlin. 'You can work your way up to that. For now, you are the big man with a bigger stick. Got it?'

Tag nodded. 'Got it.'

Emily turned to thank Master Ben for all he had done. But there was no sign of him.

'Master?' she called out. 'Where is he?'

'His work is done,' answered Merlin. 'And Ben has never been one for goodbyes. I am sure you shall see him again, sometime soon.'

CHAPTER 19

The team of hunters drove through Italy, Switzerland and Lichtenstein to get to the city of Fussen in Germany.

Tag and Troy ate their own weight in pasta in Italy, consumed almost a metric ton of cheese in Switzerland and came to a mutual decision that Lichtenstein was a good place to catch up on their MacDonald's deficiency.

Not that they didn't like the food. It was more that the food in Lichtenstein was the gastronomic equivalent of eating wood glue. The Liechtensteiner's two most popular dishes appeared to be either *Kasknopfle*, a hand grenade sized boiled dumpling made from what seemed to be paper mâché, or *Ribel*, which was a dry version of the same thing.

The team stood on the balcony of the chalet Merlin had rented for them. It was a large, log walled affair with floor to ceiling windows, hot tubs, state of the art entertainment, luxurious beds and soft furnishings. It overlooked the mountains, and the large village of Grote, situated some ten miles from the city of Fussen. Almost directly opposite them, on the other side of the valley, loomed a gigantic castle.

Schloss Heilberg. The residence of Count Frank Kraupner. Head of one of the larger German *Nosferatu* houses.

'I know it's beautiful,' said Troy. 'But for some reason I'm sick of snowy mountain vistas.'

Both Emily and Muller snorted in agreement.

'What about you, big guy?' asked Troy.

'*Om Mani Padme Hum,*' answered Tag as he held in hands together in front of his chest in an attitude of prayer.

'Seriously?' asked Emily.

'I am one with the view,' said Tag. 'Beauty is in the eye of the beholder, and as such, all looks jaded to one who is not traveling the way.'

The team stared at the big man, open mouthed.

Tag burst out laughing. 'Just trying the whole spiritual enlightenment thing on for size,' he explained. 'Personally, not sure about it. Makes me sound like a walking fortune cookie. Also, mountains, snow, bleagh. Still, hopefully the Germans got better food than those dudes who ate wallpaper paste.'

'I think you will find German food to be very much to your liking,' interjected Merlin.

'Why? What is it?' asked Tag.

'Pig mainly. Sausages, roast pork, meatballs. Also, potato. And cabbage.'

'Do I have to eat the cabbage?'

'You don't have to eat anything you don't want

to,' replied Merlin.

Tag grinned, as did Troy.

'Happy days,' noted the big man.

'When do we hit the castle?' asked Emily.

'Tonight,' answered the Prof. 'I have it on good information that the Count is having a ball. Very high society. We are all going.'

'Is it a plus one?' asked Tag.

'Why?' asked the Prof.

'Just wanna know if I can take missus Jones.'

Merlin shook his head. 'Most definitely not. It's all tuxedos, ball gowns and concealed weapons, I'm afraid.'

'Will any of those BUMF's be there?' asked Troy. 'You know, those Big Ugly Motherf...'

Merlin shrugged. 'Who knows? I hope not, although I doubt it very much. The German *Nosferatu* hate the Russians with a passion.'

'I don't want to sound like a cliché,' interjected Emily. 'But I don't have anything to wear.'

'You do,' corrected Merlin. 'As do the boys.'

'How?'

The wizard wiggled his fingers.

'That might prove to become rather annoying,' mumbled Emily under her breath.

'What about invitations?' asked Muller. 'We can't just walk up and gatecrash.'

'Actually, that is exactly what we are going to do,' said Merlin. 'All of us, including the Prof. You see, the Count doesn't require proof of invite, after all, who would gatecrash the party of one of the most powerful men in the area?'

'Us,' said the Prof.

***

Emily looked at the four men and grinned. 'My, don't you lot scrub up well,' she noted.

And to be fair, they did. Troy with his dark looks, wide shoulders and shoulder length hair. Muller's natural grace that made his muscular build seem lighter than it actually was. Tag - a tank in a dress suit. Merlin looked the business, his silver hair in a ponytail and his beard plaited into a fork.

But the biggest surprise was the Prof. Emily was used to thinking of him as a rangy, bumbling, slightly incoherent scholar. But somehow, the tux had brought out something in him. He stood straighter, topping six feet. His shoulders tapered down to a slim waist and his bright blue eyes glowed with power and otherworldly intelligence. He looked, presidential.

Troy held out his arm and Emily took it.

She was wearing a deep red, figure hugging silk ball gown with a black leather bodice over the top. A combination of Cinderella meets Goth. And it worked.

As Tag had said – she looked hot enough to fry chicken on.

Together, the team mounted the steps that led to the entrance of the castle.

A set of massive oak double doors were pushed open to allow access to the palatial entrance hall.

Guards in black leather, with long black cloaks, stood on each side of the door as well as in the entrance hall. At least twenty of them. They all carried what appeared to be ceremonial swords. But on closer inspection Emily could tell the swords were real. And it was obvious to her that every one of the guards was *Nosferatu*. Not high level, but dangerous enough.

'Blood suckers,' she communicated to Troy, using her pack link as opposed to her vocal cords.

Troy nodded. 'I know,' he responded.

One of the guards detached himself from the line and approached them.

'Greetings on behalf of Count Kraupner,' he said. 'Please follow me to the ballroom.'

The team traipsed after the vamp guard, noting the extreme opulence of the place as they walked.

They heard the music long before they arrived at the ballroom. Emily was surprised at the genre. She had expected a string quartet, or maybe even a chamber orchestra. Whatever, classical music for sure.

Instead, the strains of swing filled the air.

'The King Porter Stomp,' commented Emily. 'Benny Goodman and his orchestra. Got to number 16 on the hit parade in 1935.' She shrugged and looked slightly embarrassed. 'Sorry. Habit.'

Troy chuckled. 'Walking Google-nerd.'

The guard stopped and bowed, ushering them into the ballroom.

The place was a riot of color. Eighty or so guests

were dancing, schmoozing, drinking, talking.

The Count was immediately apparent to every member of the team. His aura made him stand out like a volcano in the Garden of Eden. A destructive force of note.

'An Ancient,' mumbled Emily.

'And a powerful one at that,' agreed Merlin. 'Everyone, stay well clear of the Count for now. He will know who, or at least what we are the moment he sets eyes on us. Let's see if we can stay under the radar for now while we check out the lay of the land. It looks like a large proportion of the people here are simply guests. I see the mayor over there, judging from the mayoral chain around his neck. Not sure who is in the know regarding the Count's real identity, and who are mere villagers looking to do a bit of social climbing.

'For the moment we shall consider everyone present as one of the enemy. Come on people, mingle with a purpose.'

Tag walked straight over to the large finger buffet, grabbed a plate and began loading up.

The Prof joined him. 'What looks good?' he asked.

Tag shrugged. 'They got loads of fish eggs. Tiny little pie things with mush in them. Stuff on little biscuits. Honest? It's all not good. What's wrong with chicken legs and pizza slices? I'm sure no one really likes this fancy-shmanshy food. Just trying to be posh instead of feeding the guests.'

He shoveled a handful of canapes into his mouth

and chewed.

The Prof helped himself to a generous mound of caviar and water crackers.

A waiter appeared and offered a tray of pink champagne in crystal flutes. Tag took one, downed it, grabbed the waiter by the shoulder to stop him leaving and then proceeded to polish off the rest of the tray, except for one flute that he handed to the Prof.

'You like champagne,' noted the Prof.

'Meh. It's fizzy,' said Tag. 'Prefer beer.'

'You, sir,' noted the Prof. 'Are a cultural barbarian.'

Tag chuckled. 'I likes what I likes.' He finished off the plate of food, handed it to a passing waiter and set off towards the dancefloor. 'Tag's gonna cut the rug,' he said. 'Time to boogie on down. I wonder if these jokers know any Reggae?'

The Prof watched the big man go, and then he scooped up another mound of Beluga.

Meanwhile, Emily found herself surrounded by men. Some young, some old.

Some human.

Mainly vampires.

She looked at the crowd of disgusting leeches around her, and for the first time since she had been turned, the tsunami of hatred didn't rise up and threaten to overwhelm her senses.

In the back of her mind, she heard Master Ben's calm voice.

'Balance. There is light, and there is dark. Both

are necessary. Remember, there is no reason to fight against that which is part of you. Accept it. Embrace it. But do not let it control you.'

Emily smiled. 'Gentlemen,' she cooed. 'I wonder if one of you might get me a flute of champagne?'

The stampede of men rushing to cater to her whim was a sight to behold.

Troy hid a smile as he strolled over to a group of three older ladies who were chatting earnestly about some inane subject. He sensed immediately that they were all human and he bowed low as he introduced himself.

'Good evening, ladies,' he growled. 'I am Troy Omega; may I enquire as to your names? I'm new to these parts, I hope you don't mind me intruding on your private conversation.'

As one, they all curtsied to him, taking in his golden eyes, flowing locks, athletic build and rough shaven appearance.

'La, sir,' gasped the one. 'I would take offence if you didn't intrude.'

The others all giggled and fluttered their eye-lashes, reduced to the state of tittering school-girls by the sledgehammer of Troy's blatant lupine sexuality.

Muller stood next to Merlin, sipping on a mineral water. Merlin had somehow managed to get a full glass of whisky, despite no one else having any.

'This lot aren't exactly suited for undercover work,' noted the Knight.

Merlin chuckled. 'No. Tag is like a massive hellhound in a suit, and as for Troy and Emily, they are both extremely difficult to ignore. You do okay.'

'Yes,' agreed Muller. 'I am a holy man. I'm used to blending into the background. The church is important, the individual is not. I must say, I am surprised you do not attract more attention.'

'I have subdued my aura,' said Merlin. 'It's a simple exercise. Ben Chu uses it all the time.'

'What do you mean?'

'Whenever he disappears,' answered Merlin. 'He's not teleporting or anything like that, he simply becomes so uninteresting, your brain glosses over him. He becomes part of the surrounds. But he's still there. Then he just walks away.'

Muller smiled. 'Crafty bugger. I thought he moved through time and space or something equally as impressive. Not some parlor trick.'

'Oh, if he needed to move through time and space, he could,' said Merlin. 'Ben is one of the more powerful beings you shall ever meet. But, on the whole, he uses what you call a parlor trick.' Merlin sighed. 'What is Tag doing?'

'I believe he is boogying on down,' interjected the Prof who had just walked over, carrying a plate full of caviar.

'I think the Count is watching him,' noted Muller.

'Not a huge problem,' said Merlin. 'He's not going to get much of a read off the big man, except for the fact that he wasn't invited.'

Sure enough, they looked on as the Count beckoned to one of the guards, calling him to his side. A quick word in his ear and the vampire guard made his way across the ballroom, heading towards Tag.

He reached Tag, tapped him on the shoulder and asked a question.

None of them heard the question, but they all heard the answer.

'I'm a friend of someone who knows one of the gatecrashers,' he blurted out.

Merlin shook his head. 'Here we go,' he said. 'There are times when I'm not quite sure if that boy is a human being, or some sort of ambulatory wrecking ball.' Concentrating on the various members of the team, the wizard pulsed out a thought. 'Prepare yourselves, the proverbial is about to hit the fan in a big way.'

The Count stood up and all about him could feel the power of his aura as he unleashed the full influence of his glamor. Some of the human guests fell to their knees as the glamor stripped their capacity to resist. Others wept openly and still more simply froze, like rabbits in the headlights.

'Bring that man here,' he boomed.

The vampire next to the big man grasped him by the arm and, applying his superhuman strength, pulled him towards the Count.

Tag didn't budge. Not an inch.

The vampire looked puzzled and tried again, this time putting visible effort into it.

Still, nothing. It was like trying to drag a mountain.

Then, with a grin, Tag allowed himself to be steered towards the vampiric Count. In fact, in a reversal of roles, as he walked and dragged the guard along with him.

Stopping in front of the Count he nodded a greeting. 'Wassuup, Count?'

'Who are you?' asked the Count.

Tag frowned. 'Who are you?' he returned.

The Count sneered at the big man. Then he beckoned to a brace of extra guards. 'Take him away.'

As they approached Tag, the Count smiled at his guests, projecting feelings of relief, belonging and contentment.

The three vamp guards surrounded Tag, two of them grabbing an arm each.

Tag smiled at them and then shook his head. 'No way,' he said. 'I don't think so.'

Troy bowed to the trio of ladies he was talking to. 'If you will excuse me,' he said. 'I think things are about to get rather frantic, and I feel I shall be involved.'

He bowed again and then moved, crossing the room in under a second to bring himself alongside Tag.

He got there just in time to observe Tag explode into action. The big man's new found speed was a sight to behold. He was faster than he had ever been. But unfortunately, he still wasn't quite as fast as a vampire.

That still didn't stop him literally tearing the arms off one of the guards before the other two hit him. One pulled out his sword and hammered it into Tag's stomach, twisting the blade savagely before pulling it out.

The second vamp drew a small, silenced pistol, placed it against Tag's wide back and pulled the trigger twice.

Troy assumed the reason the vamps were using weapons as opposed to fangs, was an attempt to keep their true identities secret from the general populace of the village.

Tag dropped to one knee.

The Count's voice boomed out once again as he flexed his glamor, using it to subdue the panicked screams and shouts of surprise, fear and disgust.

'Please, good people, be calm,' he commanded. 'Ignore what you have just seen. It is merely an uninvited guest. He is of no moment to us. Carry on with the festivities while my servants clear up.'

'Clear this up, asswipe,' grunted Tag as he stood up, grabbed the two vamp guards and slammed them together so hard the sound of the bones breaking was clearly audible across the room.

Then he pulled open his bloody jacket, drew his two Desert Eagles and shot both vamps three times in the face.

That's when the entire party went to hell in a handbasket.

CHAPTER 20

Vamp guards appeared like magic, using their blinding speed to descend upon Tag. Ten, twenty, more.

At the same time, Troy launched himself into the fray, bursting through his tux as he went full wolfman in the blink of an eye.

The Count responded by barking out a string of orders that resulted in the waiters drawing out tiny Sig Sauer Copperhead submachineguns.

Another command caused the vampire guests to instantly extend their fangs and ready themselves to join the battle.

Emily, who was surrounded by at least six vamps doing their best to woo her, called on Deathwalker and, with a flourish of her wrists, beheaded two of them before they realized what was happening.

Muller's sawn-off shotgun appeared in his hands and the double boom of its discharge thundered across the room.

The Count's eyes went blood red and his canines sprang from his mouth as he jumped high in the air, leaping towards Emily.

Half way to her, he met a crackling ball of white-hot plasma Merlin had thrown at him. It exploded with a wave of fire, burning the Count's clothes and singeing his hair. But, being an ancient, it was little more than a distraction.

Which is exactly what Merlin meant it to be.

The Count twisted in the air and landed, cat-like on his feet. As he did so, Emily was waiting. Death-walker swung, but the Count swayed backwards, lashing out with a kick as he did.

Emily rode the blow, stepping backwards as it landed, then she spun hard, bringing the double-bladed ax around in a circle, first high and then low.

The Count, drawing on his thousands of years of combat experience, evaded the attack with relative ease.

The two ultimate warriors circled each other, looking for an opening.

Meanwhile, the Prof, still holding a plate of caviar, snagged a passing waiter, ripped his sub-machinegun off him and put a quick burst into his chest. Then, with barely a pause, he lined up an-other and squeezed off a couple more bursts. Un-fortunately, the second one went a little wide and stitched its way across the mayor's corpulent gut.

'Oops,' exclaimed the Prof.

Merlin looked at him and scowled.

'Not my fault,' argued the Prof. 'Stupid thing pulls to the left. The manufacturers obviously tried to put too much gun into too small a frame.'

'Use your magic, darn it,' shouted Merlin.

'Just trying to learn something new,' stated the Prof with a huff, as he wound up a mini-tornado and sent it forth, bowling over three of the sub-machinegun wielding waiters.

No longer under the effects of the Count's glamor, the guests were running around like head-less chickens. Squawking and screaming and fall-ing down. The battle was fast turning into a circus. All it needed was a toy car full of clowns, a couple of jugglers, and a ringmaster.

Tag was using his new-found speed to full effect, dashing from one side of the ballroom to the other, shooting vamps in the face, overturning furniture, smashing glasses and generally creating utter havoc and mayhem.

He was also shouting at the same time. 'Just you wait until I get my Flame On magic. Gonna burn you all to the ground. But right now, you gonna have to settle with a bullet inna face.'

Another ten vampire guards ran into the ball-room.

'Goodness me,' exclaimed the Prof. 'There seems to be a never-ending supply of these miscreants. Well, I never.'

He launched a storm of ice shards at the newcomers. The flurry of razor-sharp ice cut the vamps to shreds. Their healing went into over-drive, but before they could fully restore them-selves, Merlin cast a swarm of miniature fireballs that rained down on them like molten hail, hissing and fizzing as they burned through flesh and bone.

Then, with a twist of his hand, Merlin pulled the molten balls to one side, cutting through the fallen vampires like red-hot scythes. With another twist, he sent them strafing back.

No amount of self-healing could keep up with the massive quantities of fiery damage the Master wizard was dealing out, and the entire group of vampires met with the true death.

Muller was using his new found strength to its full ability. After he had emptied his shotgun, three vamps immediately attacked him. Instead of drawing his sword from its concealed shoulder holster, he grabbed the first vamp by his arm and, with a mighty heave, swung him over his head and slammed him down onto the other two attackers.

'Vampire whack-a-mole,' shouted Tag from across the room. 'Nice one, Muller.'

Before Muller could answer Tag, a group of at least six more vampires dog-piled the big man and he went down in a welter of blood and torn clothing.

Troy jumped to his assistance, roaring and howling as his powerful jaws ripped into the pile of vampires.

Merlin and the Prof continued to tag-team any armed waiters, or vampires they could see.

Emily and the Count continued their dance of death. Unlike the general mayhem the rest of the team were creating, Emily and the Ancient hardly moved. There were full seconds of study and then microseconds of actual combat. Followed by another gap where they both considered each other, searching for some sort of gap or weakness to exploit.

For any normal humans watching it would seem that the two combatants would stand still, disappear into a blur for the blink of an eye and then reappear.

It was close to evenly matched.

Close. But not completely even.

Emily was just that bit faster. Just that bit stronger.

And even though the Count had hundreds of years of combat experience under his belt, Emily had her Shadowhunter training, as well as the knowledge of the Pack, handed down from member to member.

Again, and again, they clashed and withdrew. And each time they did so, blood would spray across the room.

None of it was Emily's.

Finally, the Count stopped and held his right hand up.

'Enough,' he said. 'I find myself hopelessly outclassed.' He glanced around the wreckage of his previously opulent ballroom. 'And your ham-fisted companions have destroyed my ballroom.' He pointed at a large, wrecked oil painting. It was so smashed up it was impossible to tell what it had been mere minutes earlier. 'That was a Rembrandt,' he continued. 'Painted in 1642. He gave it to me himself. This is most upsetting. I wonder, could you tell them to stop demolishing everything?'

Emily shook her head.

'Thought as much,' said the Count. 'I take it I am facing the Daywalker?'

'Yes.'

'Until now, I always thought you were a rumor. Beautiful young girl with the power of the *Nosferatu*, the strength of a werewolf and the combat techniques of a Shadowhunter. Seems rather unfair.'

As the Count talked, the battle around them slowly dwindled to a stop. Relative silence interrupted by a heaving sob from one of the few surviving human guests. Then the odd frighteningly loud boom of one of Tag's Desert Eagles as he strolled about, administering the *Coup de Gras* to any vampire who had not yet found the true death.

The Count looked at Emily and smiled. 'I don't suppose there's a chance of us coming to some sort of deal?'

Emily shook her head. And the look the Count saw in her eyes made it plain that he was already living on borrowed time.

Tag swaggered up, his tux was in shreds, and what remained was soaked in his blood. 'Hey, I'm finished shooting all the vamps inna face,' he said. 'Why don't you off this guy quickly so we can check out the rest of the place. I'm sure there must be more of them.'

The rest of the team gathered around.

The Count looked at Merlin for a few seconds and then he nodded. 'Wizard. I heard you were dead,' he said.

'The rumors were vastly exaggerated,' said Merlin.

The Count continued to peruse the team. 'Muller the Pious. The Omega wolf. Ah, greetings, Professor.'

The Prof scowled. 'Speak not to me, foul denizen of the darkest depths.'

'Same old Prof, I see,' scoffed the Count.

The Prof turned his back and walked away.

'So, what now?' asked the Count.

Muller stepped forward, a flask of Holy Water in his hand.

'The power of Christ compels me.'

CHAPTER 21

The Count died screaming.

Emily forced herself to stay and watch. It was important to her that she faced the consequences of her actions.

In a surprising display of vehemence, the Prof spat on the remains of the Ancient vampire and cursed his name.

Merlin called for calm, then he closed his eyes, concentrated and cast a spell. A visible ripple of rainbow colors spread out, like oil on water. A few seconds later he opened his eyes.

'Grinders,' he said. 'In the dungeons. At least twenty. Also, more vampires. They're spread all over the castle. Small groups, some alone. We should split up. Muller and Tag, that way,' Merlin pointed. 'Take the entire wing, start on the first floor and work up. Troy, you go that way and do the same. Emily, towards the rear of the castle. The Prof and I will tackle the center.

'But before we do, we need to get these civilians out of here.' Using a spell to raise the volume and command of his voice, Merlin addressed the few humans who had not already run from the castle.

'People,' he boomed. 'I would advise you to leave as quickly as possible. This is not over. And while I'm busy with advice, if I were you, I wouldn't bother reporting this incident to the authorities. In the past I have found that telling the police about vampires and werewolves and fire throwing wizards tends to result in little action and even less belief.' He pointed at the mayor who was currently getting some magical help from the Prof. 'Also, someone help the mayor. He appears to have suffered an injury. Get him to a doctor as soon as you can.'

The Prof looked up from his ministrations. 'Not to worry,' he said. 'I think I've sorted it. Got the slugs out and healed up the wounds. He'll be in some pain for a while, but should pull through. Eventually. I think. Maybe.'

Two middle aged men helped the mayor to his feet and walked him from the room.

The rest of the guests followed; their faces resigned. Blank with relief that for them, it was over.

One of the women Troy had been chatting to, turned to look at the wolfman. Then she smiled and waved.

Troy pulled his lips back to reveal his teeth and growled.

The woman giggled, turned and left.

Emily rolled her eyes at the wolfman. 'Really?'

He shrugged. 'Can't help it. Naturally irresistible.'

Tag laughed and high fived the wolfman.

'Okay, people,' interjected Merlin. 'A lot of

ground to cover, let's move.'

***

Emily strode through the meandering stone corridors that wended their way towards the rear wing of the castle. This was obviously an area of the *schloss* mostly frequented by the servants. Little to no ornamentation, naked light bulbs, barely enough heating to keep ice from forming on the stone.

Using all of her senses, she mentally quested ahead, seeking the presence of any other living beings. She could feel human auras. They were weak. Almost imperceptible. But further away, bright seething auras of the *Nosferatu*. Some more powerful than others.

One in particular stood out like a beacon. Oddly, although she could sense it was a vampire, it lacked the usual feeling of cruelty she associated with the average blood sucker.

One of the side doors opened and two humans walked out. Both were dressed in casual clothes, a man and a woman. They were chatting, oblivious to the mayhem that had just transpired in the ballroom.

The man looked up at Emily. 'Are you lost? You aren't allowed in this part of the *schloss*.'

'Who are you?' asked Emily.

The man sneered. 'That is my business. Now, answer my question, what are you doing here? The Master will be most displeased to find any of his guests wandering about without an escort.'

The woman, who had been staring closely at Emily, let out a gasp. 'Is that blood?' she asked, pointing at the scarlet smear running down the side of Emily's bodice.

Emily raised an eyebrow, but didn't answer.

'Is it from feeding?' enquired the woman, her voice catching slightly in obvious fear.

'Maybe,' countered Emily.

Both of the humans fell to their knees, slamming their foreheads against the cold stone floor as they kowtowed frantically.

'Forgive my tone, mistress,' groveled the man. 'I had no idea.'

'So,' said Emily. 'You know what goes on here?'

'Yes, mistress,' whined the female familiar. 'We serve at your whim. Please, we meant no offence.'

'And you are okay with the blood of innocent villagers being spent?' continued Emily.

'Of course, mistress,' answered the male familiar. 'As the Master has oft told us, they are but meat. Cattle for the slaughter.'

Emily shook her head. 'You know, I sometimes think that you familiars may be worse than the actual blood suckers. Some of them were turned without choice. But you. You chose to follow this disgusting, cruel and unforgivable way of life.'

She brought forth Deathwalker.

One fell swoop took off both their heads, and a new smear of blood was added to Emily's clothing.

She continued her search, walking down the

seemingly endless corridor, senses alert. Seeking.

Two more familiars were dispatched and one lower-level vamp before she approached the powerful aura she sensed earlier. She slowed down as she got closer, and finally, she stopped before a plain wooden door to the left of the corridor. It was exactly the same as all the other doors. Nothing fancy. No sign on it. No cleaner than any of the others.

Nothing different.

Except for the blazing aura of power that emanated from behind it.

Emily decided to go for shock and awe and simply kicked it in. The door flew off its hinges and spun across the room, smashing into the opposite wall.

Stepping in, she saw walls covered in shelves, filled with ancient tomes. On her right, a small desk. Sitting behind the desk, a slight, silver haired man, dressed in an old-fashioned three-piece suit. His hair was slicked back and he sported a small goatee beard and pencil moustache. His eyes were so pale blue as to be almost colorless.

He was obviously a vampire.

Looking up from his book, he smiled.

To Emily, the smile looked genuine. Like an uncle seeing his favorite niece who seldom calls. It was at odds with the fact she knew him to be a *Nosferatu.*

'Ah, yes,' he said. 'I wondered when you would appear. I felt many powerful auras, but yours stood out like torchlight in a dungeon.'

Emily didn't answer. Nor did she equip Death-walker. At the moment, even though the vampire exuded power, he did not project danger. If any emotion came across, it was regret.

'Forgive my rudeness,' continued the vampire, as he stood up and bowed. 'I am doctor Gunter von Bless, at your service, madam.'

Still Emily did not answer. Instead, she cautiously approached the vampire, noting his body language, deciding how much of a threat he actually was. After a few seconds she made her decision, stepped forward and sat down in the chair opposite his desk.

'Emily Hawk,' she introduced herself.

'Delighted, miss Hawk,' replied the Doctor as he sat back down. 'So, I assume after all the cessation of life I sense from upstairs, you have come to kill me.'

'You cannot kill that which has no life,' answered Emily.

'Really?' frowned the Doctor. 'What a narrow view you must have of life. *Cogito ergo sum.* I think, therefore I am. Surely that belief is certain and irrefutable.'

'I am not here to debate philosophy.'

'No, you are here to end me.'

'Not you specifically. All of your type.'

The Doctor shrugged. 'It is what you do. So, do it.' He stood up and walked around the desk.

Emily flowed to her feet.

The Doctor knelt in front of her. 'Make it quick,' he said.

Emily nodded and brought forth Deathwalker.

'You know,' said the Doctor. 'I never wanted to be a child of the night. I was turned against my will some eight hundred years ago. Unfortunately, in all that time I have been too cowardly to take my own life. Or end my existence as you would put it. So, I became a recluse. Living in the servant's quarters with my books. A life of self-exile.'

'Are you trying to tell me you are the victim here?' scoffed Emily.

'Why not?'

'What do you live on?'

The Doctor raised an eyebrow. 'You know we need human blood to survive. It is not a choice.'

'I know,' said Emily. 'I have felt it. The hunger is impossible to resist.'

The Doctor looked up at her. He smiled again. 'I thought as much. It is you. The Daywalker. So, you know of the hunger.'

'Yes.'

'And still, you wish to end me?'

'It is because of the hunger that I need to end you,' answered Emily. 'All of you. Because you are no better than a single celled organism. A virus. You have no control over what you do. You must be stopped.'

'Perhaps,' argued the Doctor. 'But have you ever...'

He didn't finish his sentence before the ax

swept down. His head leaped from his shoulders, bounced off the wall and rolled across the room.

'Enough philosophizing, you blood sucking leech,' growled Emily.

She booted the head against the desk and left the room.

CHAPTER 22

'There's no one here,' said Tag. 'Merlin gave us the fun-free zone to scout.'

'You think fighting the *Nosferatu* is fun?' asked Muller.

'Sure,' answered Tag. 'Better than dealing drugs on the streets, and fighting idiots hyped up on PCP or whatever new drug is being pushed at the moment.'

'I always forget your past,' said Muller.

'Yeah, whatever,' mumbled Tag. 'I'm doing good now.'

Muller grasped the big man by the shoulder and gave him a squeeze. 'That's what counts.'

They proceeded down the corridor, kicking open doors as they did.

'What the hell are all these empty rooms for?' asked Tag. 'Must be thirty or more. What a waste of space.'

'Maybe guest rooms back in the day. Store rooms? Who knows?'

Tag kicked down another door and then paused. 'Hey, Muller. Check this out.'

He pointed at a flight of stairs that wended

downwards. Sporadically placed wall sconces showed it continued down for at least two floors.

A stench of human waste and unwashed bodies wafted up, assailing their nostril with a fair bit of olfactory aggression.

'Stinks,' noted Muller.

'Prisoners?' ventured Tag. 'Grinders?'

Muller shrugged. 'Merlin told us to scout this floor and up. Not down.'

'True,' admitted the big man. 'But here,' he gestured around him. 'No one to fight. Down there, maybe someone to fight.'

'I think we should check upstairs first,' said Muller.

'What if they're prisoners?' asked Tag. 'Sitting in the dark, terrified. Starving. Waiting to be eaten. Surely, we should strive to rescue them as soon as possible? It's a moral imperative.'

'A moral imperative?'

'Yep. I think.'

Muller shook his head and smiled. 'Okay, big man. Lead the way.'

The two hunters descended the steps. Muller had his shotgun in his hands, and Tag sported his twin Desert Eagles.

As they got closer to the bottom, they began to hear the sounds. A combination of wailing, insane gibbering and screeching.

'Grinders,' said Muller. 'I hate Grinders.'

'Sounds like there's a lot of them,' added Tag. 'And I don't have Missus Jones with me. She loves to dance with Grinders.'

'They'll be locked up,' noted Muller. 'We'll take a look and see if we need to get the rest of the team to help.'

At the bottom of the stairway was a dark landing. One door leading off it. Thick, steel bound oak.

Tag turned the handle and, cautiously, pushed it open.

The smell hit them like a charging rhino. And now the door was open, the sound of the brain-fried vampire-spawn flooded the air.

Dim lights showed a row of steel barred cages. Each one held at least six Grinders.

There were ten cages in all.

'I reckon we go back, get some help,' suggested Muller.

'No need,' countered Tag. 'Only six per cage. We open the cages one at a time, deal with them, then go on to the next cage. Simple.'

Muller thought for a few seconds, then he nodded. 'Seems like a plan.'

Tag checked out the first cage. 'How the hell do these doors open?' he mused. 'There's no place for a key.'

'Electronic,' said Muller. 'Over there. Those switches. Each one corresponds to a specific cell. You push it, door opens, Grinders run out. We dispatch them.'

'Cool,' said Tag as he walked up to the panel of switches. He stared at them, counting left to right, turning every now and then to verify his positioning with the actual cells. 'Got it,' he announced. 'This is the button for cell number one.'

He pushed it.

There was a slight pause, and then, with a hum of electrical power, every cell door swung open.

Tag looked up.

'Oh, crap.'

CHAPTER 23

Merlin walked briskly through the central area of the house. The Prof trailed slightly behind, stopping every now and then to study a particular painting or wall hanging.

Unlike the rest if the team, Merlin didn't have to physically check room to room to ascertain whether they were occupied or not. He simply knew.

How?

Because.

'Keep up,' snapped the wizard.

'This Count fellow had a remarkable collection of art,' noted the Prof. 'I've seen two missing Degas, a Turner and a remarkably good counterfeit of one of Van Gogh's lesser-known Night Sky renditions.'

'Don't care,' said Merlin. 'There are a bunch of people in the room at the end of that corridor. Humans. Come on.'

Once again, Merlin took the lead and strode down the passage towards the room he had identified. Just before he got there, he casually mumbled a short incantation, gestured, and one of the doors leading off the passage exploded in a ball of flame.

A brief scream was audible above the explosion for a fraction of a second before the flames caused it to cease.

'Bloody amateur,' sniffed Merlin. 'Trying to suppress his aura and ambush me.'

He reached out and tried the door handle. It was locked. But the barely perceptible murmur of conversation ceased the moment he jiggled the handle.

In deference to the people locked inside the room, Merlin refrained from simply blasting the door open. Instead, he wove a more subtle spell, placed his hand on the door and released it. The door vibrated slightly and emitted a high-pitched sound, like someone running their wet finger around the rim of a crystal goblet.

After a few seconds, the door slowly crumbled to dust.

It revealed a single room. Large. Triple bunk beds bolted to the stone floor. Along the far wall, a row of stainless-steel toilets. A couple of steel basins.

Two dim, naked light bulbs gave the room a graveyard glimmer. No windows. A single exhaust fan in the ceiling hummed and clattered as it made a feeble attempt to suck the dank, fetid air from the crowded room.

There were at least ten sets of triple bunks. Thirty beds. Almost every single one was full. There was nowhere else to sit. Hardly anywhere else to even move.

A prison room from hell.

The occupants, a mixture of men and women, stared hollow eyed at the two old men who had just entered. Their despair was a tangible thing. They knew where they were. They knew what they were there for.

And they waited patiently for death.

They had become the cattle the *Nosferatu* claimed them to be.

Merlin cast a light spell, throwing a floating orb of luminescence into the air.

At the same time, the Prof conjured up a gentle wind that swayed about the room, cleansing the atmosphere and bringing with it a smell of spring-time and hope. It was a subtle magic available only to the highest of practitioners.

'Your ordeal is over,' stated Merlin. 'We are here to save you. To get you home.' His voice held the perfect blend of stern command and gentle kindness in equal measure. It was a voice that could command nations, lead armies and twist the very rules of nature itself,

It filled the prisoners with hope and courage.

The Prof's spell of cleansing, subtly healed minor wounds, slew the bulk of the filth from their hair and skin, and revitalized their flesh. It was nothing like a good meal and a safe night's sleep, but for now it would suffice. All he was trying to do was give them enough energy to leave the castle.

'People, follow me. Let us leave this foul place,' instructed Merlin. 'Professor, you take up the rear. Let's go.'

The former prisoners walked in single file behind the wizard, trusting in him implicitly.

And behind him came the Prof, spells prepped and ready to take on any comers that might threaten.

CHAPTER 24

'Umm, run?' suggested Tag.

Muller transferred his shotgun to his left hand and filled his right with his sword. 'Too late,' he said. 'Back away slowly. When we get to the stairs, they can only come at us two or three at a time. We can hold them there.'

The two hunters walked backwards, weapons pointing at the horde of twisted Grinders.

Tag pulled something from his trouser pocket.

'What's that?' asked Muller.

'Something the Prof gave me.' The big man held up a small metal orb. Dull black. The size of a baseball.

'A grenade?'

'Sort of,' acknowledged Tag. 'It's more like a smoke bomb. Except instead of smoke, it has a solution of silver nitrate. His theory is it'll burn the vamp's eyes and lungs.'

'Well chuck it, quickly.'

Tag pulled the pin and lobbed the silver-bomb into the center of the horde. It exploded with an unsatisfactory plop. More party popper than hand grenade.

But the ensuing results were a sight to behold. Purple smoke billowed from the explosion, enveloping the Grinders completely as it filled the dungeon with a thick mist.

Immediately, they started screeching in agony. Tears of blood streamed from their eyes and they began hacking up blood and phlegm. Many of them fell to their knees, clawing at their own flesh in an unsuccessful attempt to stop the burning.

Seizing the opportunity, Muller took a flask of Holy Water from his pocket, opened it and started flicking it liberally over the screeching, wailing crowd of blood suckers.

'The power of Christ compels me,' he shouted.

The Holy Water sizzled and spat as it chewed through the Grinder's flesh and bones. Stripping the meat from their skulls. Melting them with its power.

Then the booming of Tag's pistols and Muller's shotgun joined the cacophony.

At the same time, Tag started singing.

'Purple haze, all in my brain,

'Lately things, they don't seem the same.'

Then he laughed out loud. 'Man, I love Hendrix,' he yelled.

Muller reloaded, fired and then dropped the shotgun. 'I'm out,' he said as he swung his sword, taking the closest Grinder in the throat.

The two hunters edged their way slowly up the steps, firing and cutting and punching and kicking as they did so.

Below them, piles of dead Grinders littered the stairs.

'There's still too many of them,' shouted Muller. 'We've got to shut them in as soon as we get to the top of the stairs. Can't have thirty of them roaming the castle, or worse, escaping into the village.'

'Bit of a problem with that plan,' noted Tag.

'What?'

'I kicked the door down to get in, remember?'

'I do now. Damn it. What we going to do?'

'No idea,' admitted Tag. 'I'm the brawn. You're the brains.'

'Since when?'

'Since now. I'm running low on ammo. Look, when we get to the top, I'll try to prop the door in place and hold it there, you find help.'

'You mean that door?' responded Muller.

Tag glanced down at the splintered remains of what was once a door. When he had kicked it in, he had broken it into at least a dozen pieces. 'We need a new plan,' he yelled.

'Just what the hell are you idiots doing?'

Tag glanced up to see Merlin standing at the top of the stairs, a thunderous expression on his face. 'I thought I instructed you to scout upstairs. Why are you in a basement full of Grinders?'

'Because Muller didn't keep me on a tight enough rein,' answered Tag. 'So, it's not actually my fault.'

Muller scowled. 'Really?'

'Sorry,' apologized Tag. 'Brawn, not brain.'

'For heaven's sake,' said Merlin. 'Both of you, get

down.'

The two of them dropped to their knees, just as a massive fireball screamed over their heads and exploded amongst the oncoming Grinders. The heat was so intense it shriveled the hunter's eyebrows and set their clothes to smoldering.

The effect on the packed Grinders was spectacular. The superheated plasma leaped from vampire to vampire, clinging to them like napalm as it burned through their flesh, eating away at them like some sort of ravening fire-monster.

'Move it, you morons,' snapped the wizard.

Tag and Muller rose and sprinted up the stairs before the intense heat roasted them alive.

As soon as they exited the stairway, Merlin unleashed another spell. This one buzzed and crackled with some sort of blue-white electrical power. A ball of lightning. He cocked his arm and chucked it down the stairs.

The spell went off like a thunderstorm. Lighting arced across the room, shorting out on the steel bars, punching through the Grinder's flesh and turning the stone floor into bubbling lava.

When the spell finally sputtered to an end, there was not one Grinder left alive.

'Man,' said Tag. 'Why the hell do you even bother bringing us along? You don't need us. You're a one-wizard killing machine.'

'Because it's exhausting to do things magically,' snapped Merlin. 'Now come along, the rest of the team are waiting outside with the prisoners.'

The two hunters followed Merlin to the entrance, and outside.

'Where the hell have you guys been?' asked Troy. 'We heard shouting.'

'They've been playing silly buggers with the Grinders,' said Merlin. 'Decided to think for themselves instead of obeying a few simple instructions.'

'I pushed the wrong button,' explained Tag, in what was a perfect non-sequitur.

Merlin shook his head. 'Right. I've called on some help to move the prisoners. After they've been taken care of, the Prof and I are going to destroy this terrible place.'

'Do we have to?' asked the Prof. 'All of that magnificent art.'

'Yes,' insisted Merlin. 'All trace of the *Nosferatu* must be scoured from the earth. We cannot allow this to continue. It cannot live on in any way, shape or form. And that includes their ill begotten gains. It all goes.'

Four hours later, magical flames consumed the last of the *schloss*. Merlin conjured up a firestorm, and the Prof fed the flames with a vortex of wind.

Eventually, the heat rose to such a level it created its own weather pattern, pulling in more and more wind that fueled and refueled the roaring flames until they grew hot enough to melt stone.

By the end of the next day, there was nothing recognizable left.

Only molten slag and ashes.

CHAPTER 25

A person's proficiency in chess is predicted by what is referred to as an Elo ranking. The lowest end of the scale is 100. The theoretical upper end is 3000.

There has been no human being with a rating higher than 2851. At this stage one is called a Super Grand Master. In the entire history of chess there have been less than thirty Super Grand Masters.

Ali Hadad had an Elo of 3000. There is no official ranking for someone that high on the scale.

Hadad had been playing chess for over a thousand years. He found it to be the ultimate representation of a true 'Game of Thrones'.

And, as such, he had picked up on Mikael Trotsky's naïve attempts to organize a coup against the Blood King and his entourage, almost the day he had started.

His blatant courting of the guards. His childlike efforts to bring other conspirators into his fold. And his ridiculous partnership with House Romanoff.

Hadad would have been amused, if he had not been so disgusted at the awful amateurishness of

the whole affair. It offended his sense of profes-
sionalism. His love of competence.

And he was not the only one who viewed Trotsky's inefficient fumbling's with scorn. After a dis-
creet enquiry from Hadad, Romanoff himself had
turned on his potential fellow conspirator. Once
he knew the game was up, he chose to tell all and
remove himself as far as possible from Trotsky
and his clumsy efforts to usurp the Blood King's
power.

Hadad approached Jebe with all of the evidence
then stood back and watched with amusement.

He was currently sitting alongside Jebe, in a concealed alcove off the Blood King's private chamber.
They were waiting for Trotsky and his covey of
subverted guards to make their move.

Tonight was the night. In fact, Hadad had
worked out Trotsky's schedule before the traitor
had done so himself. There were only a few times
when the attempt could successfully be made. And
they depended on the allocation of the guards, the
times of day when the king was alone, and the
whereabouts of the guards who were not in Trotsky's camp.

In fact, it had been so ludicrously easy to outplay
the usurper that it held little entertainment for
Hadad. But it was better than sitting around waiting for news from Arend and his current progress
regarding the search for the *Triginta*.

Stifling a yawn, Hadad heard someone fiddling
with the outer door to the king's chamber. They

were obviously picking the lock.

Moments later, his superlative hearing dis-cerned eight distinctive sets of footsteps. The idiots weren't even capable of maintaining a de-cent level of stealth. He was sorely tempted to leap from his hiding place and yell, Boo! It would have been in keeping with the childlike level of subter-fuge offered by these idiots.

But it wouldn't do to spoil the surprise.

The group snuck across the entrance area and headed towards the king's study. They knew the king was there alone, because Jebe had ensured the information was freely available.

Kicking open the door to the private study, Trot-sky shouted.

'Prepare to meet the true death, tyrant.'

There was a pause. Then one of the guards yelled out. 'It's a familiar. In the chair. It's a familiar with a gag on, not the king.'

Jebe strode out of the concealed alcove, followed by Hadad.

They walked into the inner room.

'Ah, Trotsky,' said Jebe. 'As monumentally ineffi-cient as usual.'

Trotsky turned to face Belikov's second. 'What? I...? How did...?'

'Idiot,' snapped Jebe. 'Your ham-fisted attempt to manage a coup was laughable. Pathetic.'

Trotsky's face reflected his utter astonishment. Then he noted that the only other vampires pre-sent, apart from his guards and himself, were Jebe and Hadad.

He smiled. 'You may consider me an idiot,' he said. 'But I am not so stupid as to confront an elder warrior and seven associates with only a scholar as backup.'

'He is not a scholar,' contradicted Jebe. 'He is a philosopher.'

Trotsky sneered. 'Well, forgive me. That will make a difference, I'm sure. Can you fight, philosopher?'

'I prefer not to,' admitted Hadad.

'What a pity,' scoffed Trotsky. 'Because, unfortunately your preferences hold little sway right now.' He turned to one of his guards. 'Kill the philosopher.'

The guard blurred into motion, crossing the interceding space in microseconds.

The clash lasted less than two seconds. Bones broke. Flesh tore. Blood sprayed across the room.

And the guard lay in pieces at Hadad's feet.

'I said, I prefer not to,' said Hadad. 'I did not say, I could not.'

'You unbelievable incompetent,' noted Jebe. 'If you had paid any sort of attention in the past few years, you would know, as does everyone else in the palace, that Hadad used to be the chief enforcer for the Knights Templar. He was known throughout the entire medieval world as, *Murmur de mort*. The whispering death. As for me, I am merely here to observe. My friend,' Jebe gestured to Hadad. 'Do your duty.'

Trotsky died last.
Screaming for mercy.
It took a while.
And all the time, Hadad did not utter a sound.
Murmur de mort.
The whispering death.

CHAPTER 26

Arend had sent the latest three pieces of the *Triginta* to the Blood King's palace using a team of trusted familiars.

Then a jeweler attached the three new coins onto the growing necklace that was to eventually become the complete *Triginta Argenteous*.

Now there were six out of the thirty.

The necklace literally hummed with power. An almost imperceptible sound that vibrated at a frequency so low, it affected all around it. As one approached, one could sense one's internal organs throbbing in time to the vibrations.

It was a distinctly unpleasant feeling.

That, plus the unavoidable problem that the *Triginta* was made up of silver coins, a metal that was an anathema to the *Nosferatu*, meant that simply being in its presence set Belikov's fangs on edge.

It felt like someone was filing away his canines with a sheet of rough sandpaper.

But the converse of this discomfort was the heady feeling of power the artifact bestowed upon the wearer.

When Belikov wore the necklace, albeit over a

leather protective smock to prevent the silver actually burning him, he was almost impossible to resist.

Even Jebe, a vampire known for his mental strength and forthrightness, found that when his king was enhanced by the *Triginta*, any suggestion he made seemed to carry with it such power, such authority, perception and insight, that to deny his any wish was unthinkable.

If Belikov suggested the sky was dark green and the grass sky blue, the power gifted by the *Triginta* would make his statement seem fact. Regardless of what your eyes told you. His aura of absolute leadership would negate such trivial things such as reality.

And this not even a quarter of the artifact's full potential.

The only being not swayed by the power, was Hadad. He felt it. But he knew how to ignore it.

This was because, during his time spent with the Knights Templar, he had been exposed to many such artifacts.

A piece of the Cross.

The spear of Longinus.

Even the Arc of the Covenant.

He had never been high up enough to be shown the Grail.

The point being, over time, he and his fellow knights had been trained to ignore the powers of the Holy Relics.

But Hadad knew, judging from the power of the

incomplete *Triginta*, even he would fall to its spell when it was the complete article.

And that scared him.

'You did well,' stated the Blood King. 'Not that Trotsky and his minions would have been able to harm me, even if you had not managed to unearth their pathetic rebellion.'

Jebe bowed. 'We live to serve, my king.'

'Yes,' agreed Belikov. 'You do. And now I shall give you the opportunity to serve me again. This coup attempt, foolish and pitiable as it may have been, still concerns me. I fear that some of the other houses may be seeing me as weak. And that will not do.'

'I am sure they don't, my king,' denied Jebe. 'It was but a single misguided instance.'

Belikov held up his hand to forestall any further disagreement to his theory. 'Regardless of what you think, it is my command that you put together a strategy to bring the rest of the Russian houses to heel. Bring me the leaders of all of the houses. I will address them. I will stamp out any misgivings they may have. I will instruct them, and they shall obey. It is time to crack the whip, dear Jebe.'

Jebe bowed. 'As you command, so shall it be.'

Belikov stared at Hadad. 'And you, Arab? I note you do not genuflect. Do you not agree with me?'

Hadad raised an eyebrow and then shrugged. 'What he says,' he answered, pointing at Belikov's number two.

Then, together with Jebe, he left the room.

CHAPTER 27

The team were back in the folded space that held Merlin's mountain getaway.

'I still think we might have kept a couple of the paintings,' said the Prof.

Merlin didn't deign to answer. He had spoken, and his word was law.

'It sure made a nice fire,' noted Tag as he sat at the table, rubbing his thumb and forefinger together in an attempt to create flame.

'That's not how you do it,' snapped Merlin.

Tag looked up. 'Hey. Mister wizard,' he said, his voice calm yet questioning. 'Why you got such a bug up your ass lately? Wassuuup?'

Merlin stared at the big man for a few seconds, then he took a deep breath and let it out slowly. 'You're correct,' he admitted. 'I apologize.'

'So, what is the problem?' asked Emily as she walked over and put her hand on the ancient wizard's shoulder.

'It's those vampires,' interjected the Prof. 'Those ones you call the BUMF's. You know, the Big Ugly Man Feeders.'

'Big Ugly *Man Feeders*?' laughed Tag. 'Seriously?'

The Prof scowled. 'What?'

'Nothing,' said Emily. 'Carry on.'

'Thank you.' The Prof applied a flame to his pipe, puffed and continued. 'We have been doing a little research on them. And, quite frankly, what we discovered has us more than a trifle worried.'

'A lot worried,' grunted Merlin.

'Why?' asked Emily.

'They are members of House Belikov.'

Emily frowned. 'I don't know them.'

'Obviously,' said Merlin. 'How could you? Most of your knowledge comes from the internet, and vampires aren't much for social media.'

'I'm not sure if that was sarcasm, or just an old man being unreasonably snippy,' retaliated Emily. 'Whatever, it's basically true, so I forgive you.'

Merlin shook his head. 'I seem to be doing a lot of apologizing of late. Once again, sorry. Let me explain.'

'That would be nice,' said Emily.

Merlin explained the history of Belikov. The Blood King. And how his house was affected by the Chernobyl fallout, and his subsequent impact on the world of the *Nosferatu*.

'However,' he added. 'It gets worse. The Prof and I are not yet sure, but it seems as if Belikov is making some sort of attempt to become the King of Kings amongst the *Nosferatu*. Not only of the Russian houses, but all of them. So far, we have found no evidence involving America, but Europe and Asia seem to be involved.'

craig zerf

'I knew it,' exclaimed Muller.

'You did?' asked the Prof. 'Why didn't you tell us?'

'Well, I didn't exactly know,' admitted Muller. 'But I suspected something was going on. Too many coincidences. Too much proof of different houses cooperating. And evidence of the Russians everywhere. In fact, the only place we haven't come across any was at the Count's castle.'

'The Russian hatred for the German *Nosferatu* runs deep,' said Merlin. 'I doubt Belikov would deign to parley with the Germans. In fact, I suspect, once he has consolidated the Russian houses, he may very well declare war on the Germans.'

'Good for us,' said Troy. 'We stand back, wait to see who wins and then take out the victors.'

'You've come up against couple of the Chernobyl vampires,' said Merlin.

'Yes.'

'And you still think that the German's might be victorious?'

Troy didn't answer.

'I thought so,' continued Merlin. 'Imagine a hundred of those monstrous creatures, with Grinders, and well-armed and trained familiars. Most likely ex-Spetsnaz. Trust me, even you four couldn't stand against them.'

'We might if you stood with us,' said Tag.

'Even if Prof and I did, they would kill us all.'

'He's right,' confirmed Emily. 'It took everything I had to beat the last one.'

'Me too,' admitted Troy. 'If I was facing two, I doubt I could have beaten both of them. Well, maybe, but not three.'

'Three would be my limit,' added Emily. 'Or four. But the one I killed intimated he was far from one of the most powerful. So, I don't know. It's not good.'

'Now add the rest of the Russian houses,' said Merlin. 'Another three, four, five hundred vamps. We are in big trouble. The only thing keeping me from having a full-blown meltdown, as it were, is the fact that vampires don't play well together. Because if Belikov manages to form any sort of alliance, we are all finished.'

'Well, that's marginally depressing,' said Emily. 'What can we do about it?'

Merlin looked grim. 'Hope,' he said. 'For some sort of miracle. Pray to whatever gods you know that the Houses do not rally.'

'I have found the gods to oft be capricious and unreliable,' interjected the Prof. 'Perhaps some more practical advice would be welcomed.'

'We need to look for allies,' said Merlin. 'Both human and supernatural. If this is actually going down, basically, we need an army. And trying to convince an army of humans to fight irradiated vampires could prove, let's say, rather difficult.

'As for supernatural help, there are a few I might be able to call on, I shall put out some feelers, just in case.'

CHAPTER 28

The land of the Fae is large. Perhaps twice the size of the Earth as we know it. Perhaps even more, for it is a difficult realm to measure in purely logical terms. Space folds back on itself, time runs differently and parallel universes coexist.

Where humanity has settled on three dimensions of space; length, width and depth, and one dimension of time, Fae scholars argue whether there are twenty, thirty or perhaps forty separate dimensions. Their arguments are to string theory as checkers is to chess.

At this moment, the Morrigan and her unintended new compatriot, Balor the Cyclops, were arguing. In all fairness, in the short time the two had teamed up, the Morrigan had come to realize that Balor's default setting was to disagree.

'I have my Fomorian warriors,' he grunted. 'A full dozen of them. I know Merlin is a challenging foe, but with your skills, my power and the combined weight of the Fomorians, we can beat him. Especially if we lay an ambush. Take him unawares.

'I see no reason we need to subjugate tribes of goblins and imps and force them to assist us. It is both unseemly and unnecessary.'

The Morrigan pursed her lips. 'We need warriors. Lots of warriors. And by Fae custom, if we defeat any of the Goblin tribes, they are ours to command. The right of conquest holds.'

Balor stared at the Morrigan for a full minute as he contemplated her words. 'Talk, warrior woman,' he snapped. 'What is it you are not telling me?'

'The wizard may have some allies,' she admitted.

'May?'

'He does.'

'Who?'

'A young girl.'

Balor laughed. 'So?'

'Well, she might be … the Daywalker.'

'What?'

'And there's a werewolf.'

The giant cyclops scoffed. 'I eat werewolves for brunch.'

'Yes,' agreed the Morrigan. 'Except this one might be the Omega.'

'Holy cra...'

'And they have teamed up with a Knight of the Holy See, Muller. And some idiot called Tag.'

'Muller the Pious?' asked Balor.

'Maybe.'

'And Tag the immortal?'

'Is that what they call him now?'

'Yes, that *is* what they call him now,' answered Balor facetiously. 'On account of the fact you cannot kill him.'

'Everything that bleeds can die,' snapped the Morrigan. 'Oh yes, and that awful Professor is with him.'

Balor paled visibly. 'Morrigan,' he said in a low voice. 'We need to talk.'

'There is nothing to talk about. We need cannon fodder. And a few hundred Goblins should suffice.'

Balor shook his head. 'Maybe. But Goblins will be as chaff before the wind. With opposition like you have mentioned, we need a class of warrior far stronger. A few hundred Goblins will be as naught before the Daywalker and her compatriots.'

'What do you suggest?'

'Orcs.'

The Morrigan laughed. 'Orcs? Don't be ridiculous, Balor. No one can control them. As dumb as pigs and as trustworthy as a rattlesnake.'

'Their custom also adheres to the right of conquest,' replied Balor. 'If one of us challenges one of their chiefs to a battle and wins, that tribe must obey us for the passing of twelve moons.'

'And you could defeat their chief?' asked the Morrigan.

'Undoubtably,' answered Balor. 'However, as we are the challengers, they get the right to choose whom they fight. I have little doubt the chief will choose to face you in mortal combat, as opposed to me.'

'Why?'

'What can I say, Orcs are incredibly misogynistic. Why fight a male when you can fight one of the weaker sexes?'

'I am the goddess of war,' stated the Morrigan. 'Do you honestly think the Orc chief would be that stupid?'

Balor grinned. 'I can almost guarantee it. And once you have defeated him, each defeated tribe will give us access to a hundred plus eight foot tall, five-hundred-pound warriors with attitude.'

The Morrigan nodded. 'True, but do not forget, they are as dumb as a box of hammers.'

Balor shrugged. 'So? As you already said, we need cannon fodder, not military geniuses. We could overwhelm Merlin and his cohorts with simple numbers. As you know, in battle, quantity has a quality all of its own.'

'True. Do you know where to find the chief?'

Balor smiled again. 'I do.'

'Then lead on.'

CHAPTER 29

'What is a Sotheby?' asked Mist.

'It's an auction house,' answered Arend. 'Are you familiar with auctions?'

'I am not grotesquely stupid,' snapped Mist. 'I was simply unaware of the Sotheby.'

'Sotheby's actually, the "S" is important. Whatever, it's in London, England. We need to go there.'

'And the twins are convinced that another part of the *Triginta* will be on the block?' asked Remer.

'Nothing is carved in stone,' answered Arend. 'But their information points that way. They think it is part of a large collection. Said collection contains a few Roman Denarii, one which might be what they are looking for. The seller has no idea. You see, many scholars believe that Judas was paid with Shekels of Tyre. A common misconception, as those were the only coins accepted by the Jerusalem Temple at the time. However, most trade was conducted using Roman coin, thus, the Denarii. And if the twins are convinced, that is enough for me. After all, they are very thorough.'

'Where is this London,' enquired Remer. 'And will we have to go in an iron flying box again?'

'Nerd alert,' shouted Arend. 'What have I told you?'

'No noob sentences. Don't sound like a dork,' parroted both of the Fae.

'And what is the iron flying box called?'

'An airplane,' said Mist.

'Correct. So, what's with this flying box crap?'

Both of them shrugged.

'The next time either of you use noob nerd language again,' continued Arend. 'I am going to remove the first section of the little finger on your left hand.'

'Harsh,' mumbled Remer.

'But fair,' snapped Arend.

***

The trio of *Hulder* exited the private jet and took a cab to the Dorchester Hotel in London. The Sotheby's auction was scheduled for the next day and Arend decided to get to the city with plenty of time to spare.

Plus, he liked London. English pubs, fish and chips, Carnaby street and good cider.

He also loved the fact that the British police didn't carry firearms. Much easier to fight someone who brought a truncheon to a firefight.

That evening the three of them ate at the hotel, then Arend took the noobs to a pub in the East End. To call it a dive would have been kind. But that's how the *Hulder* boss liked his drinking establishments. Down, rough and dirty.

Arend ordered a round of Scrumpy Jack, a coarse apple cider with a kick like a cantankerous mule. To ensure they all got the full effect of the alcohol, he chased the rough drink with vodka.

'Listen up,' he said to the noobs. 'I'm going to order a few more of these, then I'm going to pick on a group of the meanest looking patrons here and insult them.'

'Why?' asked Mist.

'Because Londoner's do not take insults lying down. So, they will call me out and, most likely attack me.'

'Ooh, a fight,' interjected Remer. 'Can we kill them? Burn them? Explode their heads?'

'No,' answered Arend emphatically. 'However, we will fight them. But without magic. And I'm serious about that, you use magic, it's chopping off finger time.'

'Why?' asked Remer. 'I don't get it. What does it matter if we kill them with magic, or our bare hands?'

Arend giggled. 'No killing,' he said. 'That's the point. It's fun. We are going to fight, using fists and feet, and no killing.'

Both of the noobs stared blankly at him.

Arend shook his head. 'Trust me. I insult, they react. We all fight. But no killing. Actually, make sure you don't use any of your more esoteric martial skills. Fight as a *Hulder* child would. Be as ineffectual as possible, but still win.'

Their leader's instructions were so obscure they

left no real room for questioning. It was simply a case of, listen and do as told.

They both nodded.

'Great,' responded Arend as he walked over to the bar to get another round.

Half an hour later the three *Hulder* and five stout Londoners were having at it. Punches flew, people were thrown across the room and a small amount of blood decorated the furniture.

Another hour on, and the *Hulder* and Londoners were drinking together, toasting the Queen, singing drinking songs and slapping each other on the back.

During a pause in the loud revelry, Mist stood up and started to sing. It was a traditional *Hulder* funeral song. All about a man who died, never having plucked up the courage to tell a girl he loved her. A song about loss, desire, opportunities missed and heartfelt angst.

Her voice throbbed with passion as she sang. A lilting, almost Celtic cadence with a low husky delivery.

When she finished, there was nary a dry eye in the room.

One of the Londoners started to clap. Then they all joined in.

An old man approached her and bowed slightly. 'You have the gift, lass,' he stated, in a broad Irish accent. 'And my heart sees now what my eyes could not. You are one of the old-folk, are you not?'

Mist smiled, but did not answer.

The old Irishman nodded, took her hand and kissed the back. 'Thank you,' he said. And then he left, his face a picture of wonder and gratification.

Arend smiled benignly at all and ordered another round of drinks for everyone present.

Ye gods, he loved this city.

CHAPTER 30

Even the most exclusive auctions at Sotheby's are open to the public, and there is no obligation to bid.

However, some patrons are treated with more deference than others. One such was Lord Rupert Poncenby-Smythe, the oldest son of the recently deceased Lord Phineas Poncenby-Smythe, founder of the Poncenby-Smythe range of incontinence pants (by Royal appointment).

Phineas had started with a vast family fortune and turned it into an obscene mountain of wealth. And on his death, the title and the entire estate was left to the ministrations of his son, Rupert.

Unfortunately, Rupert was not a chip off the old block. In actual fact, Rupert was little more than a staggeringly stupid, pathetically weak, lazy wastrel. And in the past few months since his father's death, he had done his very best to squander the family fortune. As with everything else, he was unsuccessful. The staggering affluence defeated his rather pathetic attempts to spend it.

Of late, however, Rupert had managed to up his game. This was mostly due to his new girlfriend.

A Russian model of such staggering beauty that it was immediately apparent to all that the only reason she was swimming in the same pool as the aging, chinless, large eared, stick insect that was Lord Poncenby-Smythe, was his money.

And Katerina Karkoff was doing her very best to separate him from as much of it as possible in as brief a time span as she could.

In short, she was having a blast. And the few minutes a week of sweaty congress she had to endure, was a small price to pay for such largess.

Now they were at Sotheby's. They had come to buy stuff. Just general stuff. Anything she felt like. Rupert was showing off in the only way he knew how.

Conspicuous consumption.

He might have a tiny … umm … whatever, but he had a huge wallet. And woe betide anyone who tried to bid against him. He would show them, the world, and the delightful miss Karkoff, who was the king of all pins.

***

Arend had come along with enough cash to ensure he would be able to bid successfully on the lot he wanted. He could have simply taken it, but after careful contemplation he decided it was far simpler to throw money at the problem until it went away.

He took a seat near the front of the room. Mist and Remer sat each side of him. Their collective good looks attracted more than a little attention. Arend ignored it. Both Mist and Remer preened like show birds, flirting outrageously with all comers.

Arend was about to tell them off for attracting unnecessary attention, but then he decided to let them have their fun. After all, it was doing no harm.

He did notice a tall, dark haired beauty with full lips and cut-glass cheekbones looking at Mist like she was some sort of enemy. Arend hoped Mist didn't take offence, or the tall brunette might just end up being a lot less alive than she would have anticipated when she got out of bed that morning. She was sitting next to man who seemed to be made up of spare parts tied together with string. Tall, lanky, disjointed, chinless, and a laugh that made a donkey's bray seem like a mother's lullaby.

The first few lots came and went without much excitement. The chinless wonder bid for anything shiny. Gems, jewels, ornate snuff boxes. If it twinkled, the brunette would nudge him and he would stick his bidders paddle up until he won the item. Then she would simper, and he would expose his misshapen yellow teeth in what he must have considered to be a winning smile.

Finally, lot twenty-seven. A collection of rare coins circa AD 27 to 36.

Arend put his paddle up.

The brunette nudged mister chinless.

And the fun and games started in earnest.

craig zerf

The bids rose quickly through the low five figure range and into the six. At One million four
hundred and seventy thousand Pounds Sterling,
approximately two million dollars, Arend reached
his limit. He had not expected to pay more than a
million. At most.

The gavel came down, chinless gave another of
his rubble-toothed smirks and the brunette giggled shrilly.

Arend was pissed. How dare they. Bloody ... he
tried to think of a suitable insult ... humans.

He turned to Remer. 'I want those coins. We
could wait and get them after the auction, but
who knows where they may end up. So, I think we
should take them now.'

Remer grinned. 'Rules of engagement?'

'What the hell,' answered Arend. 'Go bonkers.
Whatever you and Mist want. Have fun, just make
sure you don't damage the coins.'

Mist stood up and called out to the brunette.
'Hey, tall, dark and gormless. I saw you looking at
me.'

Karkoff turned to face the *Hulder*, an expression
of contempt on her face. Everything about her
said, look at me, I am the wealthiest. My boyfriend
has more money than you.

Then her head exploded.

After that, the world went mad.

Collateral damage was the watchword of the day
as fireballs, lightning strikes and ice shards destroyed the room and everything in it.

Arend cast a shield around the box of coins in order to protect them, then he strolled through the mayhem and picked it up.

The auctioneer made a weak attempt to wrest the chest back, so Arend used a blade of ice to remove both his arms. And that stopped any further resistance. At least from him.

Sounds of police sirens pierced through the screams and wails of the wounded and the dying, so Arend figured it was time to go.

He knew he could just as easily have taken the coin chest without so much wanton violence, but he was irritated and, truth be told, had a slight hangover from the night before. Consequently, he decided to take it out on the local population. After all, they were only humans.

A group of policemen rushed into the auction room and Arend knocked them down with an exploding ball of plasma, setting their clothes on fire and searing their exposed skin.

Then he called to his two compatriots, conjured up a portal, and the three of them stepped through to appear back at his French residence.

The portal closed behind them, cutting off the sounds of violence and mayhem.

Arend opened the coin chest. It was full of graded coins, each one in its own plastic container. He stared throwing them out, briefly inspecting them as he did.

Halfway through, he stopped, dropping the box and keeping hold of the single coin they had been looking for.

It vibrated sightly with an obvious otherworldly power.

'Yes,' he said triumphantly.

'Boss,' ventured Remer. 'Can I ask a question?'

'Go ahead.'

'If you can just teleport us from place to place, why did we have to take the big iron flying box?'

Arend stared at the Fae assistant. Then he conjured up an ice blade. 'Hand,' he commanded. 'Stick your finger out.'

'Oh no, please, boss. Sorry.'

'Too late. Don't say I didn't warn you.'

The blade flashed.

The finger fell.

Remer scowled. 'Ouch.'

Shut up,' snapped Arend. 'Noob idiot. Anyway, it'll grown back.'

'I know. But it still hurts.'

'Whatever. Let's get this coin to Hadad.'

CHAPTER 31

'Take a look at this,' said the Prof as he placed his laptop on the kitchen table.

'What,' asked Tag. 'You found some videos about cats on You Tube?'

The Prof stared at the big man for a few seconds. 'Cats?'

'Yeah. Cat videos are funny. And cute.'

The Prof shook his head. 'No, not cats. This is currently on all of the major news channels. Look, everyone.'

They gathered around the computer and the Prof hit play.

It was a shaky amateur video taken by someone's cell phone. The picture swayed from side to side and jumped frequently as the camera person ducked and dived while still attempting to get footage of the ensuing mayhem happening around them.

In the background, fireballs careened across the room. Wind vortices ground their way through the chairs, throwing them aside and smashing the resulting wreckage into people. Hundreds of razor-sharp shards of ice ripped and tore through human flesh.

The cacophony of explosions was almost loud enough to drown out the screams and wails of the wounded and the dying.

'*Hulder* battle magic,' said Merlin.

'Yes,' agreed the Prof as he slowed the video down. 'Look, here, here and here. There are three of them. These two are doing the real damage. This one seems to merely be watching.'

'What's he doing now?' asked Emily.

They all watched as Arend strolled over to the auctioneer, cut his arms off and took a small chest from him.

'Man,' said Troy. 'These psychos are hard core.'

'Yes,' said Merlin. 'The *Hulder* are known for their cruelty. They find violence amusing. Death and torture are a hobby to them. They revel in destruction.'

The sound of approaching police sirens intruded.

'Here come the coppers,' noted Tag.

A thin strip of light appeared in the video. Then it expanded into a doorway and the three *Hulder* jumped through. As soon as they did so, it disappeared.

'Teleportation,' said Merlin. 'Damn. There are very few mages powerful enough to do that.'

'You can,' observed Muller.

'Yes, I am one of the very few,' answered Merlin.

'I think it is Arend,' offered the Prof. 'The image is of atrocious quality, but I recognize his tells. The way he conjures. I'm pretty sure it's him. The other two, no idea. Just your run of the mill *Hulder* warrior-mages.'

'Arend,' mused Merlin. 'What would bring that nightmare out into the open. For the last hundred years or so, he's been concentrating primarily on scholarly pursuits. We need to find out what was in the chest he took. That should give us a hint.'

'Already done that,' said the Prof. 'It's a collection of rare coins circa AD 27 to 36. Here,' he flicked to another tab on his laptop. 'This is a list of them.'

Merlin scanned the list. 'Nothing out of the ordinary here,' he concluded. 'Do you have any theories?' he asked the Prof.

The Prof frowned. Then he took out his pipe and proceeded to carefully pack it.

All knew this was a habit of his when he was preparing his thoughts. A physical manifestation of the anxiety he was feeling.

Finally, pipe set to his satisfaction, he lit it with a gesture and puffed it to life.

'I do have a theory,' he said. 'And I hope to all of the gods it is felonious.'

'Well, shoot then,' urged Merlin.

'Amongst the coins in the chest, one was a Roman Denarii. A silver one. Now, this may seem like a bit of a flyer, but bear with me. You see, after some sifting through various sources on the internet, I discovered that this is not the first robbery that may have involved magic. Particularly *Hulder* battle magic. There have been various reports of some serious atrocities. Mass murder and proof of fire, wind and ice being used on the victims. In Germany and on some isolated island cult dwelling.

'Strangely, there have also been reports of a bizarre incident at a place known as The Farm. A French Foreign Legion training facility. Not entirely sure what that was all about, but it may be linked.

'Whatever, that's not important, what is important is that this theft is part of an ongoing trend.

'Have any of you heard of the *Triginta Argenteous*?'

'Yes,' confirmed Merlin, at the same time the rest of the team offered their denials.

'For those of you ignorant to the facts, I will summarize. You all know the story of Judas, the disciple who sold out Jesus for thirty pieces of silver.'

There was a general mutter of assent.

'Good, the *Triginta Argenteous* is the name given to those pieces of silver. Thirty Roman Denarii. It is said that an artifact was created from the coins and that artifact gives the owner immense powers.

'From what I know, and I have studied this in some depth over the last few centuries, there is no such artifact. One may have existed at some stage, but fairly soon after Judas's death, the coins were split up. I won't go into the details, suffice to say. They do exist and even singularly, they are capable of extending great powers to their owner. As a full set, their power will be off the charts.

'There are many different theories as to what those powers might be, but the general consensus is the *Triginta* imparts powers of leadership. I am talking serious leadership capabilities. The one who wields the *Triginta* will evoke worship, love, reverence and devotion from whomever they choose as their followers. They will be impossible to resist.

'However, it also comes with a curse. In that the user will die an early death. It basically drains it's owner of their life force.'

'Well, surely that's a good thing?' offered Emily. 'So, any evil person who uses it is going to die. Problem solved.'

The Prof nodded. 'True. But what if the owner was already dead?'

'Then that won't be a problem,' said Tag. 'On account of them being not alive... oh, crap.'

'You see what I'm saying?' asked the Prof.

'Yes,' said Tag. 'What if the owner is a vamp? Then there is no life force to drain. You would have an eternal, really bad, blood sucking king of the world.'

'The Russians,' snapped Muller. 'Does this have any link to the Blood King and his attempt to expand his empire?'

'I think so, yes,' answered the Prof. 'I suspect that Belikov is collecting the coins that make up the *Triginta Argenteous.* And if he does, he will be unstoppable. Millions upon millions will die, and the rest of humanity will be enslaved. They will become little more than cattle for the *Nosferatu*.'

'We have to stop him,' said Emily.

'So, no pressure then,' quipped Troy.

'How about I make us all a nice cup of tea,' said Tag. 'I'm sure things will all seem a lot better after.'

CHAPTER 32

'You mentioned The Farm,' said Muller.

'Yes,' affirmed the Prof. 'I heard there was an incident involving what could only be described as monsters. They took out a score of Legionnaires. Eventually one of the Commandant's exterminated them.'

'Did you get a name, by any chance?'

'I believe it was, Swanepoel. No first name.'

Muller grinned. 'That would be Commandant Quinton Swanepoel. Recipient of the Military Medal, Cross for Military Valor, and the *Legion d'honneur*.'

'So, you know him?'

'We have fought alongside one another a few times,' confirmed Muller. 'Before I got involved with the church. I would like to speak to him, hear exactly what happened.'

'I have had dealings with the Legion in the past,' interjected Merlin. 'I know Brigadier General Jean Lardet. Well, I am more a family friend than a personal friend of the General. I will accompany you.'

'We'll all come along,' said Emily.

Merlin shook his head. 'No. I will be teleporting

the two of us. Over that distance, it would be impossible to take anyone else. Even with just the pair of us I will be pushing the limits.'

'Fair enough,' conceded Emily. 'When are you going?'

Merlin glanced at Muller.

'I'm ready to go at any time,' said the Knight.

'Soon,' replied Merlin. 'I have something I'd like to discuss with the Prof and then we'll be off.'

'What do you need?' asked the Prof.

'Latobias,' answered Merlin.

'The Celtic god of wind,' said the Prof. 'What about him?'

'Can you contact him? Ask if he can help us?'

The Prof frowned. 'He is easy to contact. After all, the wind is everywhere. But I'm not sure if he will answer. You know how flighty he can be.'

'He has helped us before,' noted Emily.

'So? That means nothing,' said the Prof. 'As I have oft said, the gods are capricious. They make decisions using information we are not privy to. And their thinking defies all human logic. It happens when you think in millennia, not years or lifetimes.'

'You and Merlin are old,' pointed out Tag.

'Yes,' agreed the Prof. 'And do we think like you do?'

'Point taken,' admitted the big man.

'Anyway, in answer to your request,' the Prof said to Merlin. 'I shall do my best.'

'That is all I can ask. Now, Muller, stand next to

me. Oh, and this is a long jump, so, you may feel a little ill. Try not to throw up on me when we land.'

'As if,' mumbled Muller as he stood next to the wizard. The air shimmered and bolts of electricity crackled about the room.

Then they were gone.

CHAPTER 33

The wizard and the Knight shimmered into existence directly outside the main gate to The Farm.

'Well, that wasn't so bad,' said Merlin.

Muller swayed slightly, placed his hands on his knees – and threw up everything he had ever eaten. Ever.

Merlin waited patiently for the Knight to finish, and then he patted him on the back. 'Better out than in, I always say.'

At that moment, two armed sentries rushed up, brandishing their rifles.

'*Arrêt*,' shouted the one. '*Ne bouge pas.*'

'Evening, fellows,' said Merlin by way of greeting. 'We're here to see Brigadier General Jean Lardet.'

'Where did you come from?' asked the sentry as he scanned the area, picking up not sign of transport, nor any fresh tracks leading to the gate.

Merlin wiggled his fingers.

'Don't,' urged Muller. 'These Legionnaires are notoriously lacking in humor. 'He turned to the sentry. '*Pardon, monsieur, veuillez appeler le général ou le Commandant. Dites-leur que* Muller, *le Chevalier du Saint-Siège est ici.'*

The sentry's look of concern immediately changed to one of awe. 'Muller the Pious?' he asked.

Muller scowled. 'Yes. The selfsame one. Now run along, we have little time.'

The sentry threw up a smart salute, turned on his heel and ran.

The second sentry stood to attention. 'If you and the old man could wait here,' he asked respectfully. 'I am sure the General will be along shortly.'

'Old man?'

Muller chuckled. 'Well, you are a million years old.'

'Not true, I'm only been around for a couple of millennia. Old man? Bah! I should turn him into a frog for that.'

'Can you? I mean, are you able to, that wasn't a request.'

'Of course. You want to see?'

Fortunately for the sentry, Merlin's demonstration was cut short by the arrival of the first sentry and another man.

'Muller, you SOB,' the newcomer shouted.

'Quinton, you useless peon,' replied the Knight.

The two men hugged, laughing loudly as they did.

'And who might this be?' asked Quinton.

'This is my good friend, Merlin.'

Quinton shook the wizard's hand. Then his expression changed from joy to apprehension as he took in Merlin's appearance, his silver hair, his violet eyes and his obvious aura of great power.

Before he could speak, Muller nodded. 'Yes,' he said. 'That Merlin.'

'*Merde*,' cussed the Legionnaire. 'Are you still caught up in that otherworldly, saving us all from the apocalypse, religious crap?'

Muller nodded. 'That's why we're here. Heard that some of that crap went down right here on The Farm.'

Quinton nodded. 'Something definitely did. Come with me, you will need to speak to the General.'

They followed the Commandant through the gates and into the camp.

***

'Those monsters that killed my men were vampires, you say?' mused the General. 'What were they doing here?'

Merlin shrugged. 'No idea. Jean. We know they are searching for a certain artifact. But I don't think that was tied up with their visit. It may simply be they were lost. Or working on false information.'

'And you are sure that these vampires are looking at world domination?' continued the General.

Merlin nodded. 'I know it sounds the height of some insane conspiracy theory, but it is what it is. I personally have been fighting the *Nosferatu* for many centuries. It is a war that never ends. Your father knew all about it, I am surprised he didn't tell you.'

'He hinted,' replied the General. 'To be honest, we weren't close.' He leaned back in his chair, steepling his fingers. 'Commandant,' he continued.

'Sir,' answered Quinton.

'Put together a team of ten men. The very best. It looks like the Legion is about to go into the vampire killing business.' He looked at Merlin. 'I assume you were going to ask for our help?'

Merlin smiled. 'Actually, yes, I was. Thank you.'

'Our family is still indebted to you,' answered the general. 'And as the leader of the Legion, this is also now my family. So, it is the least I can do. Also, it is the job of the Legion to combat evil, whatever form it may take. We will need a day; give me an address, and I will send the men to join you as soon as we are ready.'

Both Merlin and Muller stood up. The four shook hands and Quintin showed them to the door.

'Is there anything else?' he asked.

Muller shook his head. 'No, thank you. I'll see you when I see you.'

'Not if I see you first,' laughed Quinton.

'Peasant.'

'Reprobate.'

The air shimmered, lighting crackled.

The wizard and the Knight disappeared.

Quinton shook his head. 'Weird.'

CHAPTER 33

Muller threw up again.

Then the two men walked to the front door of Merlin's hideaway and let themselves in.

As always, they went straight to the kitchen that was the hub of the home. The rest of the team were seated around the kitchen table, drinking from steaming mugs of tea. With them was someone Muller had worked with before.

The newcomer stood up and bowed slightly. 'Merlinus Ambrosias Myrddin Wyllt, I greet thee.'

Merlin bowed low, a much deeper genuflection than that paid to him. 'Latobias Noricum, patron of sky, mountain and wind, I greet thee.'

Then the two stepped forward and hugged each other, both with broad grins on their faces.

'I thought you may not come,' said Merlin.

Latobias shrugged. 'The Professor called, and I was but ten minutes away, so I came. The team have explained what is happening. The situation seems dire.'

'Very much so,' confirmed Merlin. 'We have just been visiting the French Foreign Legion, they have tasked a team to help us.'

'That is welcomed news,' said Latobias. 'I too can think of a few who may be of help.'

'Gods?' asked Emily.

Latobias nodded. 'Yes, but the deities I am thinking of have fallen out of favor of late. I think this situation may be just the sort of thing to help them get back into the game.' Turning to the Prof, the god continued. 'Can you organize me some transport. If I am to help, I will need some sort of aerial conveyance, for while I can travel anywhere, the rest of you shall need a physical means to do so.'

'Of course,' replied the Prof. 'Any specific requests?'

'I like helicopters. See if you can fetch me an Airbus H175 Supermedium, or a Bell 525 Relentless. Either will do nicely.'

'I'm on it,' confirmed the Prof.

'Do you need my bank details?' asked Emily.

The Prof shook his head. 'No need. Merlin has more money than most countries. He won't even notice the cost.'

'Man, must be nice to be rich,' said Tag.

The Prof turned to the big man. 'Do you want some money? Give me your account numbers and I'll throw a couple of million in if you like.'

Tag grinned, then shook his head. 'Nah, I don't even have a bank account. And anyway, what would I do with all that money? As long as you guys keep me in shirts and suits, and provide unlimited ammo for missus Jones, I'm good. But thanks for the thought, Prof. Seriously, that was a real nice offer.'

***

The Airbus was delivered to a nearby address the next day. Which just goes to show how massive amounts of cash can make anything possible, even rush orders on state-of-the-art helicopters.

Latobias transported himself to the helicopter and then flew it back, guiding it into the area of folded space that contained Merlin's hideaway with ease. One of the obvious benefits of being a deity.

'Can you pick up some people for me?' Merlin asked him as soon as he touched down.

'Sure.'

'The contingent of Legionnaires. Do you need coordinates?'

'No,' replied the god.

'How long...wait, sorry, I know. Ten minutes each way.'

Latobias chuckled. 'Ten minutes. As always. I'll get going now. Will they be ready?'

'I'll make sure they are.'

'So, we getting ourselves a private army?' asked Tag.

'Pretty much,' replied Merlin.

They went inside to get something to eat. Just over forty minutes later, the sound of the helicopter landing rent the still mountain air.

The team went outside to greet the new arrivals.

Quinton deplaned first, followed closely by nine

more Legionnaires, all heavily armed and fully kitted out.

'I thought you said we were getting an army,' said Tag, disappointedly. 'There's only ten of them.'

Quinton heard the big man and grinned. 'Ten Legionnaires is an army, my friend.'

'He speaks the truth,' said Muller. 'Trust me.'

Tag raised a skeptical eyebrow. 'We'll see.'

CHAPTER 34

Master Ben Chu leaned on his oaken staff and studied the ten Legionnaires, his expression blank. Unreadable.

The soldiers stood at rigid attention, staring straight ahead.

Finally, the Master turned to Merlin. 'Yes, I will train these men,' he said.

Commandant Quinton Swanepoel frowned. 'Permission to speak?'

Ben nodded.

'We are the French Foreign Legion, sir,' said Quinton. 'We go through one of the most rigorous training regimes in the world. And this team of men are the very best of the best. With all due respect, sir, I doubt there is much you can teach us when it comes to combat.'

'I see,' returned Ben, his voice soft. Almost regretful. 'Well then, French Foreign Legionnaires, prepare yourselves for battle.'

None of them moved.

'You heard me,' snapped the Master.

'Do it,' yelled Quinton.

The legionnaires moved from attention into

different stances of preparedness, fists ready, well balanced, prepared for combat.

There was a flurry of snow, like a miniature whirlwind, accompanied by the solid sound of oak striking bone and flesh.

Less than three seconds later, every Legionnaire, including Quinton, was lying in the snow, clutching various parts of their body's.

'Training starts tomorrow morning at sunrise,' said Ben. 'You will report dressed in trousers only. No shirts, no shoes.'

Then he disappeared.

Quinton struggled to his feet and stood, swaying slightly as a trickle of blood ran down his face. 'That,' he said weakly. 'Is one mean old leopard-man.'

***

'We need to go to Pareen,' said Latobias, referring to the magical Fae town that existed under the city of Paris. 'I think we can safely leave the Legionnaires here, under the less than gentle auspices of Master Chu and the Commandant.'

'Any reason?' asked the Prof.

'One of the gods I mentioned is there. She will need a bit of convincing, and for that, one needs a personal touch. I think the whole team should accompany me.'

'Slight problem there,' interjected Emily. 'They don't allow werewolves or vampires in. Troy is a werewolf and, technically, I'm both. The cats will sense us and go mental.'

Emily was talking about the thousands of felines that lived in the Fae cities. They were encouraged to stay there, as they were the perfect sentries and alarm systems for any werewolf or vampire intrusion. Both supernatural classes had long been banned from the Fae cities, since their constant warring spilled over and started resulting in collateral damage.

'Yet you have both been there before,' stated Latobias.

'Yes,' admitted Emily. 'Sylvian taught me a way of covering my aura and extending that cover to those around me. But I have grown in presence since then. My aura is much harder to conceal. As is Troy's. He was a simple pack member when we last went. Now he is the Omega. I doubt I could shield the both of us.'

'Probably not,' confirmed Latobias. 'However, I can.'

'Are you sure?' asked Emily.

The Celtic god stared at her and, just for a split second, unshielded a mere trace of his power.

Emily looked away. 'Sorry,' she apologized. 'Of course you can.'

'Get ready everyone,' said Merlin as he turned to face Tag. 'And before you ask, no. Missus Jones is not invited.'

Tag pouted. 'Not fair,' he mumbled. 'We's like Billy Shakespeare's, Romeo and Judy, ours is a forbidden love.'

'Juliet,' corrected Troy.

'Whatever.'

The big man stomped off to collect his gear.

CHAPTER 35

As always, when flying with Latobias it took them ten minutes to reach a private airfield just outside of Paris. From there they used a chauffeur service to take them to the Pantheon Monument in the Sorbonne area of the city.

They debussed and followed Latobias to the rear of the monument. There was a single door, slightly recessed into the stone wall. No visible sign of lock or handle, and the door itself was fitted so tightly one would be unable to slip even a hair around it.

The Celtic god placed his palm against it and with a sigh of escaping air it swung inwards. Walking inside he beckoned them to follow him.

'Not looking forward to this,' said Tag.

'Why?' asked Latobias.

'The forty gazillion steps,' answered the big man. 'Both boring and tiring. Not to mention, dark.'

Without replying, Latobias led them to another door. He opened this one in the same way. But instead of revealing another corridor, this one gave access to an ancient, steampunk looking elevator.

There were no buttons donating the floors. Instead, a series of polished brass levers, wheels and valves took their place.

'Is this safe?' asked Tag.

Latobias didn't answer. He waited for all to enter, then he proceeded to spin wheels, pull levers and open various valves. Steam billowed out, and a low whistle issued from the valves. Then, with a violent lurch, followed by a series of squeaking shudders, the brass and steel cage plummeted downwards at such a pace that everyone became momentarily weightless.

Seconds later, the cage slowed down so quickly, they had to flex their knees to absorb the deceleration.

'No stairs,' said Latobias in a deadpan voice.

The door rattled open and they were greeted by the spectacular vista that was Pareen.

It was even more beautiful than Emily remembered it to be. Most likely because this time she wasn't under threat, running from vampires and fighting for her life.

The thousands of crystal stalactites reflected the innumerable balls of magical lights that floated across the cavern. Shades of warm white, light blue and even the odd yellows and reds, all refracted by the crystal into dazzling rainbows. The fragrance of heather and roses and fresh cut grass filled the air, even though Emily could see no sign of any of the aforementioned.

As before, the general hubbub of the city, shouting vendors, street musicians and arguing business people, was all underpinned by a low throbbing hum. It took a while to realize that the droning swell and fall of noise was in fact the sound of the thousands of cats. Sitting in groups on street corners, running across roofs, climbing pillars, winding around people's legs as they walked. Tabbies, gingers, grays. Persians, short hairs, rag dolls and pavement specials, all purring constantly.

The city's living alarm system.

'Fear not,' said Latobias. 'None shall detect your aura. Nor that of the Omega.'

They followed the god down a long flight of stairs and through the central market. Many of the Fae greeted him, most bowing as they did so, paying him obvious respect. Surprisingly, just as many did the same to both Merlin and the Prof.

'We're in exalted company,' said Muller.

'Yeah, well, we pretty high and mighty too,' returned Tag. 'The Pious, the Immortal, the Daywalker and the Omega.'

'Try not to announce who you are to the entire population, my boy,' advised Merlin. 'After all, that would destroy the hard work Latobias has undertaken to conceal your identities.'

'Oops, sorry,' apologized the big man. 'Just tourists,' he continued loudly. 'Nothing to see here. Normal folk going about their daily business. Except for the god, and the two really old guys.'

'Tag,' snapped Merlin.

'Boss?'

'Shut up.'

'Yes. Sorry again, boss. Just trying to allay any

suspicions.'

Merlin looked away, trying his best not to chuckle.

They continued to follow Latobias through the sprawling underground city. Slowly, the areas they walked through became noticeably less salubrious until after thirty minutes or so they were in a part of town that could only be described as low-budget.

There were less magical lights. More shadows, and more things lurking in the said shadows. Buildings were more ragged looking, unkempt and unwashed.

Loud music blared out of some of the establishments, and small fires burned on street corners.

'Who would have thought areas like this existed in a magical underground city,' noted Emily.

'Areas like this exist through necessity,' said the Prof. 'In all cities throughout the world, no matter how far back in time you go, there is always a cesspit. An area where the detritus sinks to the bottom to collect. You cannot get rid of them, as they provide a necessary outlet.

'Granted, they also provide a Petri dish to culture violence, theft and various nefarious doings, but they will always be there.'

'Where are we heading, and when are you going to tell us who we are meeting?' asked Merlin.

Latobias pointed ahead. Open double doors. Two tall humanoid doormen, both clad in full armor, massive broadswords slung across their backs.

'Rough looking place,' commented Troy.

'We're going to meet, Sirona,' added Latobias.

'Really?' questioned Merlin. 'That skanky old witch? What for? Her powers of late have dwindled to a level that is less than impressive.'

'She is not a witch,' answered Latobias.

Emily noticed Latobias didn't deny Merlin's, *skanky* comment. 'What, or who exactly is Sirona?' she asked.

'Goddess of thermal springs,' answered the Prof. 'Fallen out of favor lately, given that not many people worship thermal springs anymore.'

'Did they ever?' asked Troy.

'Oh yes,' confirmed the Prof. 'The Romans considered her a healing divinity. She was always big in the Nordic countries. Any place with geysers or hot springs. Even the Victorians gave her a nod. Nowadays, it's only the lunatic fringe. And gods tend to reflect their worship. So, yes, Sirona has tended towards the flakey of late.'

'What powers does she have?' asked Emily.

Merlin sniffed. 'Water based powers. Not that she has much left. Can shoot jets of water. Heat it up, good for making a cup of tea, I suppose.'

'She can also increase the mineral content of water,' added the Prof. 'Tends to make the water smell of rotten eggs.'

'Okay,' said Emily. 'So, not much then.'

'Also mixes a mean cocktail,' said Latobias. 'But judge her not on what she has become, judge her on what she once was, and what she may be again.'

He led them past the doormen and into the bar.

It was a single, large room. Dim balls of light floated above the various groups of tables. A goblin was playing a lute and singing. Well, Emily assumed it was singing, although it sounded more like a man quietly wailing in either agony, or terminal remorse.

A long bar ran down the one end.

And serving behind it was a woman. Maybe six foot three tall. Thin and willowy with eyes so pale blue it was disconcerting. Almost transparent so the orbs looked white with a black dot in the center where her pupil was. She had applied her makeup with a heavy hand, dark kohl around her eyes, savage slashes of shiny, bright scarlet lipstick, matted layers of mascara and stripes of rouge on her cheeks.

But even with all that, the most noticeable thing about her was her hair. Long and black as coal, it swirled about her with a life of its own. Rising, falling, billowing from side to side, exactly like seaweed being buffeted about by the sea.

The entire ensemble made her, not beautiful, but mesmeric.

The team followed Latobias up to the bar. There was a selection of other customers, some at the bar, some sitting in the chairs, being served by waitrons.

Even the smallish show of patrons contained more species than Emily had come across before.

The Prof, sensing her curiosity, leaned forwards

and spoke under his breath. 'Far table, that's a mountain troll,' he informed. 'Huge, cantankerous. Seldom seen in Pareen, must be here for a specific reason. That table over there, *Hulder*, you might call them elves. Whimsical creatures, vain and unpredictable.

'Humans over there, strange that, seeing so many together. Oh, look there, a Hobgoblin, the fellow with the sparkly blue skin, sitting with those other normal goblins. Very rare. Basically, goblin royalty. Hence the larger size, finer features. Very touchy, don't stare at him, they tend to go off at any perceived insult. And they literally perceive anything as an insult.'

'Hey, sparkly skin guy. Is that natural or do you put, like, glitter on or something?'

Emily and the Prof turned to stare at Tag, who was busy looking at the Hobgoblin, an expression of genuine interest on his face.

The Prof rolled his eyes.

Emily shook her head. 'Sometimes it's like being in charge of a six-year-old.'

'What are you doing?' snapped Merlin.

Tag frowned. 'Nothing, just asking shiny-man if his sparkle is natural.'

'You have insulted me, human,' roared the Hobgoblin, as he stood up, wielding a short, wide-bladed spear.

Tag looked honestly baffled. 'Why? How?'

'Your mere presence offends me. And even though I was munificent enough to ignore your fetid existence, you decided to hurl insults at me and question my heritage.'

'Not true, blue-guy,' argued Tag. 'I don't give a crap about your heritage; I was simply asking about your twinkly-ness.'

The Hobgoblin stepped around the table and approached the big man. Pound for pound, the Hobgoblin was actually larger than Tag. Taller, broader and more muscular.

He flourished his spear. 'I demand satisfaction.'

'Whatever,' responded Tag. 'I demand loads of crap. The company of missus Jones for one, but you think anyone gives a damn? No. Not fair, is it?'

The Hobgoblin stopped dead, baffled by Tag's apparent non sequiturs.

'Who the hell is missus Jones?' he asked, drawn into the conversation despite himself.

'Exactly,' answered Tag. 'It's like she doesn't exist to them. Makes me so mad sometimes. And I don't care that she's so heavy, and needs two car batteries to work. Or even that her ammunition is so expensive. We got a good thing going, missus Jones and me.'

The Hobgoblin started to talk, then stopped, then started again as his brain caught up with the conversation, and then simply decided to ignore it.

'I demand satisfaction,' he repeated.

'Tag,' said Merlin. 'Try to handle this without making too much of a scene. And by that, I mean killing him would be creating a scene.'

Tag nodded. 'Okay, mister-sparkles,' he said as he

took off his jacket and then unbuttoned his shirt to expose his chest. 'There you go, you can stab me with your little spear. That make you feel better? Then me and my pals can carry on.' The big man turned to Merlin. 'And you will owe me another shirt.'

'Fair enough,' agreed the wizard.

The Hobgoblin stared at Tag for a few seconds, then with a howl of anger he lunged forward and stabbed the big man in the center of his chest. Twisting the blade viciously, he withdrew it and stood back.

Tag dropped to one knee with a grunt of pain, stayed still for a moment and then stood up, the wound already closed. 'Hey, check that out,' he said proudly. 'I managed to keep all the blood off my clothes. Shows some skills that.'

The Hobgoblin gawked at Tag, then he looked closely at his spear, checking the blood coating it, then back at Tag. Finally, he reverted to type. 'I demand satisfaction,' he yelled again.

'Oh, sod off,' said Tag as he stepped forward and swung a mighty right hook. His fist connected with the side of the Hobgoblin's head with a sound like a melon dropping on concrete. The blue skinned entity flew across the bar, smacked loudly into the far wall and slumped unconscious to the floor.

There was a collective impressed sigh from everyone watching, as the big man's obvious superhuman speed and strength became apparent.

The rest of the goblins, who looked as if they were about to provide back up to their leader, decided that discretion was the better part of valor, and instead they picked blue-boy up and exited without a sound or backward glance.

'What a strange dude,' said Tag as he buttoned back up. 'Nice sparkles though.'

'Hey, Latobias, is that you?' yelled the barmaid.

'Yes, Sirona, as you well know,' answered the god.

'You are not welcome here. And neither are your friends.'

'Just a few minutes of your time, Sirona,' answered Latobias. 'Please hear me out and then we'll go.'

'Fine, but there's a two-drink minimum.'

'Since when?'

'Since now. And I get to decide who drinks what.'

'Okay,' agreed Latobias as they all bellied up to the bar.

Sirona cast her eyes over the team. 'Myrddin Wyllt,' she greeted Merlin. 'Professor.' Then she looked the rest up and down. Finally, she smiled. Or more accurately, leered at them. 'My, what a sexy bunch of almost humans,' she commented. 'If my powers serve me correctly, it's the Immortal, the Pious, the Omega and the Daywalker.'

'That's what I said,' blurted Tag. 'But then Merlin told me to shut up.'

'He would,' replied Sirona. 'He's such a prig. Never mind, would you like me to kiss you better?'

she licked her lips lasciviously.

Tag looked down and shuffled his feet, pushing a few cats out of the way as he did..

'Oh, how sweet,' chuckled. 'I've embarrassed you.'

'Enough, Sirona,' said Latobias. 'Serve us our required drinks so that we can talk.'

Sirona pushed a couple of cats off the counter, placed a row of shot glasses down and then, with a mere gesture, she floated two bottles of clear liquid over to her. The tops unscrewed themselves and a mixture of the two liquors gushed into the glasses.

'Impressive,' mumbled Muller.

'If you think that's impressive,' she said. 'You should see how bendy I am. I can scratch my nose with the back of my knees. Now drink up, have your say and then please leave.'

The team tossed back the two shots each.

Sirona made a moue of disappointment when none of them flinched or showed any discomfort at the industrial strength alcohol.

'What did you expect?' asked Latobias. 'This is not a normal collection of beings. Did you honestly think a bit of liquor could cause any discomfort?'

Sirona shrugged. 'Can't blame a girl for trying. Darn, even trolls choke when they down a shot of that stuff. Anyway, pay up and talk. Quickly, time is money.'

Latobias slid a small gold coin across the bar. 'We go to war,' said the god of wind without preamble. 'The *Nosferatu* are allying under the auspices of the

Blood King and they seek the destruction of the human race.'

'And?' asked Sirona.

'That isn't enough to pique your interest?'

'The humans stopped being my concern many centuries ago.'

'It won't stop there,' interjected the Prof. 'You know the *Nosferatu* have long held a hatred for the hidden cities and their occupants. If they subjugate humanity, where do you think they will strike next?'

'If that comes to pass, then I shall fight them.'

'We're wasting our time here,' snapped Merlin. 'And at any rate, what earthly need would we have for a goddess who is fit only for pouring drinks, heating water for tea and making springs smell bad? Come on, let's go.' Merlin made as if to leave.

'You insufferable SOB,' yelled Sirona. 'You know nothing. You have always been obsessed with this war against the vampires. Ever since I can remember it's been the amazing Merlin against evil. Well let me tell you, wizard, you are no great shakes yourself. You have lost almost as many battles as you have won. Begone, petty magician, you disgust me.'

'Hey, water woman,' said Emily.

'Sirona turned to face her.

And Emily delivered a cracking slap across her face.

The entire room went silent.

'You dare to strike a god?' whispered Sirona.

'No, I dare to strike a petty, vindictive has-been who is too cowardly to join the battle because she has lost her way. A timorous ex-someone who is more interested in wallowing in self-pity than actually getting her head out of her ass and doing something.'

Sirona visibly flinched at Emily's tirade. 'You know nothing, child,' she hissed. 'I was once revered. Worshipped by millions. The entire Roman Empire left me offerings and sacrifices. And now? The fickleness of humanity repulses me. Where are my worshipers now? Where is the love? The adulation?'

'Lady, you got some serious issues,' interjected Tag. 'People's worship don't matter. Who cares who prays to who, or what they sacrifice? Evil is evil, and those who stand for good don't need a reason to fight it, they do it because it's the right thing to do.

'This whole team here, they fight the good fight and no one cheers them on. No one even knows that we do it. When we die, there won't be no state funerals or lines of mourners. Hell, the fights we get into, most likely there won't even be a grave.

'But we don't care. We do it because we can. And if you are the only one capable of doing a job, then you gotta be some serious lame brain to walk away from it.

'And another thing, I make the best cup of tea in the world, and I would be honored if you were there to help me.'

Sirona stared at the big man for a while.

No one spoke.

Then she said. 'I can do more than make tea, Immortal. For I am Sirona, beloved of Apollo, Guardian to the waters of the Danube, sister of the Roman Empire, Great goddess of the Celts, healer of the sick and mother of plenty.

'Thank you for opening my eyes.' She bowed to Tag. 'I too will be honored to brew tea with you.'

She turned to face Latobias. 'So, windy,' she said with a slight smile. 'Looks like we're putting the band back together.'

CHAPTER 36

'I can't believe it took us ten minutes to fly to Arizona,' said Emily. 'That's five thousand three hundred and ninety-three miles. It's impossible.'

'Yes,' agreed Merlin. 'It is. More so when you consider we didn't need to fill up with avgas either.'

The helicopter's rotors wound slowly down, and the churned up desert dust sank back to earth. About a hundred yards from their landing spot stood a small, ramshackle cabin. The windows were unglazed and the door hung open on broken hinges. Outside, a windmill creaked sullenly in the meager wind, drawing water from a deep well.

There was no sign of life.

The eight hunters, including Sirona, deplaned and wandered towards the cabin. As they approached, a thunderous roar echoed across the surrounding monolithic red rocks that reared up from the valley floor.

'Get off my land, you fudging, pieces of sugar.'

A humanoid figure appeared from behind one of the rocks. He was around six feet tall, but the large antlers growing out of his head stretched his height to almost eight feet. He carried a massive sledgehammer in his right hand and he swung it as he walked, treating the fifty-pound piece of metal as if it were a light cane.

'Belenas?' asked Merlin, turning to Latobias. 'Seriously? I thought we were scraping the bottom of the barrel before,' he continued. 'No offence meant,' he said to Sirona.

'Offense taken, you vainglorious piece of crud,' quipped Sirona as she rolled her eyes.

'Who the hell is, Belenas?' asked Emily.

'God of laughter,' answered the Prof. 'Used to be huge. Now, comedians, movies, drugs, they've all stolen his power. Dissipated it.'

'How? I would have thought the more laughter the better for him,' said Emily.

'You'd think,' admitted the Prof. 'But they no longer worship *him*. Instead, the people worship the actual performers. The comedians themselves. The movie stars. The tweeters and instagramers. Back in the day, no one worshiped the common bard or the court fool. They laughed at them, but the reverence and devotion was reserved for Belenas. Now, not so much.'

The god strode up to them and stopped, jaw jutting out in a pugnacious fashion, arms akimbo, eyes squinted in anger. 'What the gosh darn are you people doing here?'

'Hi, Belenas,' greeted Latobias. 'How goes it with you?'

'Pee off, wind-boy,' snapped the god of laughter. 'You're not welcomed here. And you know darned well how I'm golly fudging feeling. I'm depressed. Have been for over a century now. Oh, hello, Sirona.'

'Greetings, Belenas.'

'He's got horns,' blurted Tag. 'Even if he comes with us, he can't exactly hang around, everyone will notice his horns.'

'They are not narfing horns, you son of a bucket,' snapped the god of laughter. 'They are antlers. And anyway, people can't see them. Not human people at any rate.' He turned to Latobias. 'Seriously, what are you doing here? And especially with these two shuzzbutting troublemakers,' he gestured at Merlin and the Prof.

'We have come to rescue you from your life of quiet desperation,' interjected Sirona. 'But before we tell all, how about you offer us a seat and something to drink, or has your lack of humor affected your good manners?'

'Galloping gremlins, Sirona. Don't be such a nasty hobknocker, you know I hate company.'

'Well?'

'Okay. You thirsty? Follow me, I got beer.'

A few minutes later they were all sitting around a table drinking flagons of surprisingly good, chilled lager, while Latobias laid out the current events for Belenas.

The rest of the team, besides the gods, Merlin and the Prof, couldn't exactly concentrate, on account of the fact that the inside of the ramshackle, falling down log cabin was vast compared to the outside. It was also incredibly luxurious and featured running streams of water, verdant foliage in a variety of pots, carpets, chandeliers and works of art on the pristine white walls.

And a very well stocked wet bar.

As Latobias talked, Belenas gestured casually and a bowl of peanuts appeared on the table. The team helped themselves to them, passing them around.

Emily noticed that however many they took from the bowl, it remained full.

At the end of Latobias's explanation as to why the hunters were there, Belenas shrugged. 'This has little to do with me,' he said. 'I live alone. The fate of the world does not affect me. Even if the *Nosferatu* take over, I will still be alone. No more followers. And depressed.'

'This may be a stupid question,' said Troy. 'But, do you have to be the god of laughter? It's just that it seems a pretty general theme. You know, like the god of talking, or breathing. Can't you, sorta, I don't know. Specialize?'

'I'm a god,' replied Belenas. 'I can do whatever I want. But I have always been the god of laughter. That is what I am, have been and will be.'

'Yes,' insisted Troy. 'But, why?'

'Because.'

'Because why? Seriously, I'm not trying to be obtuse. Why? I mean, for example, you carry that huge hammer, why can't you be the god of hammers?'

Belenas looked shocked. 'That's Thor's job. And let me tell you something, young dillweed, you don't mess with Thor. Okay, granted, he's sort of in semi-retirement at the moment, but no.'

'Hold on,' interjected the Prof. 'The boy might be onto something here. Brigid was the goddess of healing, later she changed and became the goddess of metalworking. It can be done.'

'She was the Dagda's daughter,' said Belenas. 'When the head of the pantheon is your father, all things are possible.'

'If you is always sad, why don't you become the god of depression?' asked Tag.

Belenas shook his head. 'No, that would be …'

Everyone thought for a while.

Finally, Sirona said. 'There is no god of depression.'

'I'd have no followers,' said Belenas.

'So?' argued Tag, in support of the Omega's idea. 'You got none now, and you is miserable anyways. I tell you, being depressed is big nowadays. Everyone is always complaining about how bad they got things. It's like, trending, you know.

'Plus, you would get the chance to hit some vampires inna face with your big hammer,' concluded the big man.

Belenas didn't smile. But his face took on an expression that was a little less destitute than it had been before. He nodded. 'Duck water and fudge berries,' he said. 'I'm going to do it. Let me get some gear and I shall meet you at Latobias's flying chariot.'

The newly minted god of depression left the room, and the team of hunters went outside.

As they walked back to the copter, Emily spoke. 'I have to ask,' she said to Merlin. 'What's with all the fudge and sugar and stuff?'

Merlin chuckled. 'Belenas abhors cuss words. He finds them uncouth and not befitting a god of laughter. So, he substitutes.'

'Yeah, but all the time. He can't finish a sentence without fake-cussing. And mostly we know what he's actually saying. I mean, fudge, sugar.'

'Sure,' interjected Tag. 'We know when he says fudge he actually means, fu...'

The copter started up, its massive engines drowning out the rest of the big man's statement.

Belenas exited his huge but small cabin, ran over and climbed in.

'Let's go,' he boomed. 'Feels good to be doing something again,' he admitted as he patted Tag on the back. 'Cheese wizz, it's great to be depressed. Thank you, young man.'

'You're welcome,' answered Tag. 'It's always a pleasure to help someone feel ... worse. Better? Whatever.'

The helicopter thundered skywards, ten minutes away from its next destination.

CHAPTER 37

'Can't we just fly there?' asked Emily.

Merlin shook his head. 'No. Nor can we take any of our modern weapons. You must understand, we are entering a different realm. A separate universe that runs on different rules. Magic is all encompassing. Technology is almost non-existent.'

'And, when we enter the land of the Fae,' added the Prof. 'There are certain rules you must all obey. Never accept a favor from anyone. Never give them your full name. Do not have sexual congress with anyone. And, finally, realize that life and death is viewed differently to the Fae. Duels to the death are a frequent occurrence, umbrage can be taken for the most obscure reasons and one must make every attempt to be courteous and soft spoken. There is much power lurking there, and you do not want to be on the receiving end of it.'

'Look, it's simple,' interjected Merlin. 'Tag, don't be an idiot. Now, are you ready?'

'Why me?' asked Tag. 'I always try my best to be polite. It's practically my middle name. Well, actually, my middle name is Cuthbert, but if anyone calls me that, I'll smack them inna face.'

Emily patted the big man on the arm. 'He just means, think carefully before you speak, that's all,' she said. 'You know, we all need to follow Merlin's lead, keep quiet and try not to attract attention. That's all.'

'Okay, fine,' said Tag. Slightly mollified by Emily's explanation. He adjusted the large battle axe strapped to his back and nodded. 'I'm ready.'

'Latobias,' said Merlin. 'If you could.'

The god of wind nodded and, with a complicated gesture, opened a rift between the here and the now. A portal to another dimension.

The land of the Fae.

Latobias had chosen a fairly remote spot for them to enter. On the edge of a forest, close to a range of snow-capped mountains.

Judging by the level of the rising sun, it was early morning, even though they had left home in the midafternoon.

'As you know,' the god of wind said. 'We are here to make contact with, Grannus. He is the god of shiny things.

Emily snorted. 'Well, I can see why he fell from grace. Who the hell worships shiny things?'

'You would be surprised,' answered Latobias. 'Long, long ago, people oft put a shiny rock in their cave and treated it with reverence. Later, you must have heard the expression, diamonds are a girl's best friend. Lots of people worshipped shiny things.'

'True,' admitted Emily. 'But not so much anymore, I reckon. Now they worship the money or the fame that led to getting the shiny stuff. Weird.'

'Come on,' said Latobias. 'There is a fair bit of walking to do. I know Grannus's vague whereabouts, but we shall need to ask around to pin him down.'

The team followed Latobias as he walked along a barely discernable track.

'Where we going?' asked Tag.

Latobias pointed ahead, towards the foot of the mountain range.

No one else spoke for the next hour as they simply trudged forward. After breasting a small hill, a village came into view, some two miles away. Latobias adjusted their track, veering towards it.

The village was typical, right out of every fantasy book Emily had ever read. A ten-foot-tall wooden palisade wall surrounded it. Four guard towers, one on each corner.

Sturdy wooden gates, manned by a pair of sentries kitted out with leather armor, small shields and spears.

'The village of Undervale,' said Latobias as they approached. 'Large enough to carry a couple of good inns, a market and a small detachment of guards controlled by a local sheriff. Oh, and by the way, they think I am a traveling bard. Same name, so don't gainsay them.'

Everyone mumbled agreement.

'Tag,' stressed Latobias.

'Hey, I'm subtle,' bemoaned the big man.

'Yeah, as a lightning strike,' joshed Troy.

The two guards threw a lazy salute at Latobias when he walked up.

'Bard,' greeted the one. 'Welcome back. Got any new material?'

Latobias laughed. 'Why, you tired of the old stuff? It's classic, the new stuff is all crap.'

Both of the guards laughed along with him. 'True, tell them what they know,' agreed the guard. 'Keep the punters happy. Who are your companions?'

'Just a group of traveling mercenaries,' answered Latobias. 'Thought I would hang out with them while crossing the mountains, what with all of the bandits about.'

'Makes sense. The entrance tax had gone up,' continued the guard doing all of the talking. 'Three coppers per person now. Bloody queen, more greed than sense.'

'Jacoby,' gasped the second guard. 'Talk like that will have you swinging from a gibbet.'

'Nah,' denied Jacoby. 'Latobias is good.'

Latobias pulled out a leather pouch and handed over two silver coins. 'Keep the change, friends.'

This time the guards gave him a proper salute.

Again, Latobias took the lead, wending his way through various cobbled streets, past Tudor-style timber framed houses, taverns and shops.

'The guards looked human,' noted Emily.

The Prof nodded. 'They do, but they are most definitely not. The guards were both lower cast

Fae. You can tell the difference between the casts with ease. The higher casts are taller, finer features, willowy figures.

'The lower casts are incapable of wielding magic. Well, not strictly true, they can, but only small amounts. And even that is frowned upon. Not illegal, per se, but not encouraged.'

'I don't get it,' interjected Muller. 'I thought the Fae were elves.'

Merlin chuckled. 'Don't say that word in this realm. What you are referring to are the *Hulder*. Humans make that mistake often. They think of the Fae as *Hulder*. And while this is partly true, all of the residents do refer to themselves as the Fae. But the actual Fae are a specific race. They are split into two realms, the Winter Fae and the Summer Fae. The realm is also physically divided as such.

'Then each faction is further split into two separate casts, lower and upper. You stay in the cast you were born into. It's pretty restrictive, but that's the way it is.'

'What part of the realm are we in now?' asked Troy.

'Summer,' replied Merlin. 'The Winter kingdom begins at the ridge of that mountain range. The range, called the Dragon's Spine, runs the breadth of the land, dividing the two kingdoms.'

'Here,' said Latobias. 'This is the inn we shall be staying in.'

Emily looked up at the sign. "Hogshead Tavern and Inn".

They followed the god of wind through the open front door, straight into the tavern.

Once again, Emily felt like she was taking part in some serious cosplay. Rushes and fragrant herbs covered the flagstone floor. Roughhewn tables and chairs, a solid wooden topped bar against the far wall, and a selection of patrons ranging from obvious laborers to silk clad merchants.

She also noticed, judging from Merlin's descriptions, none of them appeared to be higher cast.

When she mentioned that to the wizard he nodded. 'True. The higher casts would never be seen in an establishment such as this. Fae who put in an honest day's work make them uncomfortable. However, you will see the odd *Hulder*, on the whole they are a touch reclusive, but they do mix with all.'

'What about goblins, trolls, all those other species?' asked Emily.

'The same tend to hang with the same, and the different with the different,' quipped Merlin. 'Trolls, goblins, Orcs, mostly found around the more mountainous parts of the realm. Strictly speaking, they control their own kingdoms, but practically, they fall under the auspices of the Fae royals.

'The *Hulder* however, definitely rule themselves, and no Fae royal would dare gainsay that fact.'

Belenas elbowed them aside as he bellied up to the bar. 'Ale,' he bellowed, slamming his meaty hand down on the wooden top. 'Large flagons of it.

Lots.'

'Do you have any wine?' asked Sirona.

'Poo on a stick, woman,' yelled the god of being depressed. 'Troll bogeys to wine, it sours the stomach and leaves one with a foul disposition. Ale, barkeep. And a round for everyone in the house, on me.'

'Thank you, sir,' responded the barman. 'Most generous.'

'That's me,' agreed Belenas. 'Generous to a mothersmoking fault. Latobias, pay the man, I find myself temporarily financially embarrassed.'

The wind god shook his head and paid up. As he was doing so, he discussed hiring rooms for all for the night, again paying from his seemingly endless purse.

The team picked up their ales and found a large enough table to sit at.

They had only just sat down when a waitress walked over. She was holding a lute.

'Latobias,' she said. 'Potchermen was hoping you would play for us.'

'Potchermen?' asked Troy.

'The landlord,' answered Latobias. He stood up and took the proffered instrument. 'Sure,' he said. 'But only one song.'

The waitress squeaked in excitement as the god walked to a small raised dais in the corner of the room.

A hush descended on the crowd as they all turned in their seats to look at Latobias, and a general whisper of anticipation swept the room.

Then Latobias began to sing.

It was more than simple lyrics and music.

It was the score to every listeners life.

It was the beginning, and the end, and all in between.

It was life, and it was death.

It was laughter, and it was weeping.

It was the joy of victory, and the harsh pain of defeat.

It was the gentle caress of a summers breeze.

It was the destructive force of a winter storm.

It was the voice of a god, and all who listened heard it with their very soul.

Emily found, to her astonishment, that she was weeping openly. And when she looked about her, there was not a dry eye in the room.

Slowly, one by one, people stood and started to applaud. Until the entire room was on their feet, stamping and clapping and shouting.

One of the gods had sung.

And it was good.

CHAPTER 38

The next morning the team gathered in the common room to break their fast.

Both Troy and Tag were eating massive steaks with a side order of fried eggs. Everyone else settled for bread and honey. Except Belenas who had ordered mead and was dipping his bread into it.

Emily shook her head. 'Really?' she asked. 'Mead for breakfast?'

'It's made from honey, so there's no fiddle sticking difference between what I'm having or what you are,' argued the god of depression.

'I spoke to the landlord last night,' said Latobias. 'He thinks Grannus is living in, or near, a village up in the mountains.'

'No worries then,' said Troy. 'After brekky we'll take a hike and go find him.'

'The village is called, Grzwaklsnok,' added Latobias.

'That's a bit of a mouthful,' said Emily.

'Not if you're a troll,' returned Latobias.

'Oh, snot on an acorn,' grumped Belenas. 'A frigging troll village? I hate trolls.'

'Why?' asked Muller.

'Everyone hates trolls,' interjected Sirona. 'On account of they are foul-smelling, vile, aggressive and almost terminally stupid.'

'And they tend to eat humans,' added Belenas.

'Hopefully, Grannus is living near the village, not in it,' said Latobias. 'Then we can bypass the trolls completely. We shall set off directly after all have broken their fast.'

***

It took almost two hours of fast walking to reach the general area of the village of Grzwaklsnok. Latobias halted the group far enough away from the settlement to observe whilst remaining under cover.

They were high enough up the Dragon's Spine mountain range to be in the area of permasnow, but after the training that Master Chu had imposed upon the team, the cold no longer bothered them.

Obviously, the gods, Merlin, and the Prof were also impervious to mere changes in temperature.

'He's there,' said Latobias.

'Where?' asked Merlin.

'That cage, in the square. Look closely. Looks like a pile of unwashed clothing in the corner. That's Grannus. The trolls are keeping him locked up.'

'How?' asked Emily. 'I thought he was a god.'

Latobias shrugged. 'Who knows? Grannus is a strange character. The best way to find out is go and ask.'

'There will be a fight,' stated the Prof. 'It's inevitable.'

'I was hoping to avoid that,' admitted Latobias. 'But if it comes to that, I'm sure we won't have a problem besting them. If they follow tradition, they will issue a challenge to one of us. They fight, we win, and that's that. Still a little puzzled as to why Grannus is allowing them to keep him in an exposed cage like some sort of animal.'

'It's because Grannus is like some sort of animal,' offered Sirona. 'Let's be honest, he's awful.'

'Oh, well, let's go,' said Latobias.

The hunters stood up and made their way towards the trollish village.

As they approached, a crowd of twenty heavily armed trolls rushed out to meet them.

'Man, these buggers are almost as ugly as the BUMF's,' noted Tag.

'BUMF's?' questioned Sirona.

'Yeah, Big Ugly Moth...'

'Weapons out,' commanded Merlin. 'Look as intimidating as possible. Troll's respect physical force, nothing else. Tag, take the lead, I think dealing with these things may fall into your particular area of expertise.'

The big man drew his massive battle ax and stepped forward. 'Tag got this,' he said as stood firm, feet astride, jaw set pugnaciously, a slight smile on his face. 'That's why they call me, mister diplomacy.'

The trolls halted in front of him, the rear ones

bumping into the one's in front, many of them falling over each other. An avalanche of flesh, armor,
massive wooden clubs, and stupidity slowly rum-
bling to a halt.

Up close, the trolls were even more massive than
they seemed at a distance. The shortest was seven
feet tall and as wide as a wagon. The biggest, over
eight feet. They all wore mismatched steel and leather armor and carried humungous wooden clubs
fashioned from tree trunks. Some had steel spikes
imbedded in them, others were adorned with simple iron studs.

None carried a shield.

Shields were for wimps.

'What you do on our land?' asked the largest
troll. 'We no invite you.'

'We invited ourselves,' answered Tag.

The troll spokesman frowned. 'How can invite
yourself? Not allowed. Troll land. You leave now.'

'Not going to happen,' returned Tag. 'We've come
to talk to the pile of rags in the locked cage over
there.' He pointed at what they suspected was
Grannus.

The troll shook his head violently, spraying out
bits of drool as he did. 'That not pile rags. That
thief. We lock him up. No food. Only water. Punish
him.'

'Oh well, his punishment is over now, we need
him. So, stand aside or I'm gonna get medieval on
your ass.'

'My ass?'

craig zerf

'Yes.'

'Why? What my ass done?'

'It's just an expression,' said Tag.

'Is stupid expression. Your ass stupid.'

Merlin suppressed a chuckle. Tag was getting some of his own medicine as he attempted to conduct a conversation made up of random thoughts and non sequiturs.

'Hell, this is going nowhere,' snapped the big man. 'Look, I challenge you to combat. If I win, we take the bundle of rags. If not, we leave.'

The troll nodded. 'Is good plan. No ass involved.'

'Could you please shut up about ass?' asked Tag.

'Okay, but you started it,' grumped the troll.

Tag started to limber up, swinging his ax back and forth to loosen his shoulder muscles.

'What you do?' asked the troll.

'Getting ready.'

The troll shook his head. 'We no fight you. You made challenge. Rules say, I choose who I fight.'

'Seriously?'

'Yes,' confirmed the troll. 'It is seriously.'

'Okay, who do you choose?'

'I choose fight little girl,' he pointed at Emily and laughed.

'That's unfair,' observed Tag.

'Don't care fair,' said the troll. 'Me fight little girl.'

'I mean, it's not fair on you,' said Tag. 'Trust me, you do not want to fight Emily.'

'Tag,' said Merlin. 'Let him fight who he wants. Just hurry things along, we don't have forever.

Places to go, vampires to kill and all that.'

The troll looked puzzled. 'Very old man no care we kill little girl?'

'I've about had enough of this old man crap,' snapped Merlin.

'You are relatively old,' interjected the Prof.

'So are you.'

'Yes, and I am not denying it.'

'Whatever. Emily, front and center. Kill this idiot and then we take Grannus and go home.'

'Do I have to kill him?'

'All fight is to death,' said the troll. 'Less is cowardice. Get ready to die, little girl.'

Emily stepped forward, bringing forth Deathwalker as she did.

The troll raised his massive spiked club high.

But before he could bring it down, Emily had already swung her ax twice.

There was a shocked hush as the huge troll's head slid slowly off his shoulders. Then his bifurcated body split in two and fell apart.

One of the other trolls walked up and, using his club, pushed at the big troll's remains. Then he nodded. 'He is dead. Little girl wins fight. You may take thief person.'

Latobias stepped forward. 'Thank you,' he said. Then he led the team into the village, towards the locked cage. 'Grannus,' he shouted as they approached. 'It is I, Latobias. I sally forth with Sirona, goddess of the healing waters, and Belenas, former god of laughter, now the god of not feeling very happy.'

'God of being depressed, by gosh and cheese whiz,' interjected Belenas.

'Yes, that,' acknowledged Latobias.

The pile of unwashed laundry stirred, coughed wetly, snorted and stood up.

It was the widest man Emily had ever seen. Also, one of the shortest.

Grannus stood a touch under four feet tall (or short). But the most remarkable thing about him was his breadth of shoulders. They were almost as wide as he was high. Arms like tree trunks with boulders attached and legs like church pillars. His unkempt beard hung to his navel and his hair stuck out like the proverbial haystack.

She could also smell him from where she stood. A sour blend of body odor, unwashed clothes, reeking feet and stale alcohol. It literally made her want to retch.

He could have used skunk spray as a cologne and it would have been a marked improvement.

Scratching busily at his nether regions, he stared baleful at the whole team.

Then he belched.

'Bugger off,' he rumbled. 'Lousy bunch of has-beens and do gooders. Leave me alone. Ha,' he addressed Belenas. 'You think you're depressed, you incompetent fake-sweary moron. That's nothing. Try walking in my shoes for a couple of hundred years, I'll show you depressed.' He belched again, then looked at Merlin and the Prof.

'Wizard. Professor,' he greeted them. 'Got any liquor on you, I've run dry?'

The Prof delved into his jacket pocket, took out a small pottery flask and threw it to the god of shiny things.

He caught it, pulled the stopper off and took a tentative sniff. 'What is it?'

'Rubbing alcohol.'

Grannus shrugged. 'That'll do.'

He downed the flask in one, shuddered and tossed the empty back. 'So, what are you lot doing here?' he asked Merlin.

'Usual stuff,' answered the wizard. 'Saving the world, killing vampires, same-old, same-old.'

'We're getting the band back together,' said Sirona.

'Sirona, you're an idiot,' snapped Grannus.

But Emily saw his eyes belie his utterances as he looked at the tall, goddess with genuine affection.

'Listen, Grannus,' Sirona continued. 'Are you in, or out? You can lie here in your own filth, wallowing in self-pity, or you can do what Belenas and I have done. Suck it up and get back in the game. Come on, you filthy dwarf, what's it going to be?'

'I'm not a dwarf,' denied the god of shiny things. 'You lot are simply abnormally tall. As is almost everybody else.'

Sirona stamped her foot.

'Okay,' conceded Grannus. 'Don't have a thrombosis. I'm in, got nothing better to do anyway.'

'Wait,' said Emily. 'I'll ask one of the Trolls to

fetch the key.'

'No need,' said Grannus as he grabbed two of the thick steel bars and pulled. They deformed in his hands like wet noodles as he parted them and stepped through.

Even Tag was impressed at the god's casual display of strength. The bars were as thick as a man's wrist and even the big man would have had to put in some serious effort to pull them apart like that.

'I don't get it,' said Troy. 'If you could get out at any time, why didn't you?'

Grannus shrugged. 'You ever been bored before, boy?'

'Of course,' confirmed Troy.

'Try being bored for a few centuries. You start doing the darndest things to relieve that feeling.'

'So, the god of shiny things,' noted Emily.

Grannus looked at her. 'What?'

'Nothing, just saying. Apart from your prodigious strength, what else can you do?'

'I can refrain from asking stupid questions, child,' snapped Grannus. 'And that is only one of the things I bring to the party.'

'Grannus can control light,' said the Prof. 'It's a part of the whole shiny thing worship.'

'Control light?' questioned Muller.

Grannus sighed, lifted his right hand and unleashed a white-hot ray of light. It impacted one of the ramshackle huts, causing it to burst into flames.

'Hey,' shouted one of the trolls. 'Stinky man

burns my house down.'

'Dammit,' cussed Grannus. 'Here,' he called out to the newly homeless troll. 'Have some shiny things.'

A small pile of diamonds appeared at the troll's feet.

'Ooh – shiny things,' he said. His temporary homelessness forgotten and forgiven in favor of his new-found wealth.

'Come on,' said Grannus wearily. 'I've had enough of this. Let's go.'

'Hold on,' interjected Sirona. 'One thing, just before we go anywhere.'

She gestured and a waterfall of fragrant water cascaded down on Grannus's head, scouring him clean and eliminating his foul stench.

'Blasted woman,' he yelled. 'Do you have any idea how long it took me to develop a proper stink?'

'Tough,' replied Sirona. 'From here on out, Grannus is coming up smelling of roses.'

'Bitch.'

She laughed. 'I love you too.'

CHAPTER 39

The newest hotel in Las Vegas boasted a wall of currency they called the *Hundred Million Dollar Wall*.

It was a collage of various types of currency used throughout the ages, ranging from a single Solomon Islands Rai Stone – a massive limestone disc weighing in at over a ton, through to Chinese Qi knives, Mongolian Tea Blocks, Katanga Crosses, Mesopotamian Golden Shekels, Silver Dollars, every form of paper currency that ever existed. And – three Silver Roman Sestertii.

Was the combined value of the currencies worth a hundred million dollars?

Perhaps, if one adjusted it all according to inflation.

But probably not.

However, it made for great selfies and was exactly the sort of thing that Vegas was famous for.

To Arend – the answer was yes. Those three coins were worth every bit of a hundred million.

Once again, the cyber twins had proven their almost supernatural ability to track things down.

In all fairness, over the last two weeks, Arend and his two compatriots had chased down three false leads.

An art installation in Baden Baden.

A private collector in Holland.

And a safe deposit box in a bank in Sweden.

All three of the leads had resulted in them finding silver Sestertii.

But none of them had been a part of the *Triginta*.

These three coins, however, were the real deal. Arend could feel the power throbbing through his system, even from behind the silken rope that kept onlookers back from the exhibit.

Now he simply had to figure out how to get his hands on them.

There was the obvious option. Full scale, over the top magical violence. But he knew that this was not London, England. The police here carried guns. As did most of the private security. And a good deal of the local population.

So, although it was indeed an option, it was definitely a last resort.

'Should we blast everyone and take the coins?' asked Remer in a stage whisper.

Arend sighed. Seriously, sometimes it was dealing with a hyperactive infant. And no amount of finger trimming seemed to make any difference. The moment the digit grew back, Remer forgot the point of the lesson.

'Idiot,' breathed Arend as he turned and walked away from the wall. 'Shut up and follow me. Both of you.'

He headed for the exit, gesturing for the door-man to hail a limo as he did. It was time for some out of the box thinking.

***

Tommy Little was living it large.

Ten years ago, he had risen to the top of the hier-archy in the tough world of Las Vegas petty crime.

He had achieved this in two ways.

Firstly, he never treaded on the big boy's toes, staying clear of gambling, protection, prostitution and grand theft auto. Instead, he controlled the bottom feeders. King of the pickpockets. Mugging, petty theft, begging and shoplifting were his ports of call.

And, secondly, he and his 2IC, Bill – just Bill, no second name – used a disproportionate level of violence to enforce their will on all who entered their orbit.

Criminals who trespassed on their patch suffered broken limbs and fractured skulls. Tommy saw this as a necessary part of his business model.

Bill, however, was keen to visit pain upon any-one for pretty much any reason whatsoever. His job involved a surfeit of violence, and he was a man who loved his job.

Now both Bill and Tommy were experiencing things from the other side of the desk, as it were.

Arend had decided that he would use the petty

gangster to provide a diversion while he and his purloined the *Triginta* coins from the wall.

'Stop whimpering,' Arend scolded Bill. 'After all, it will grow back.'

Tommy stared open mouthed at the *Hulder* mage. 'No, it won't.'

Arend frowned. 'Oh yes, I forgot. You people don't regenerate.'

Bill was currently curled up on the floor in the fetal position, mewling softly, the ruined remains of his left hand clutched to his chest.

You see, Bill had blundered.

When Arend introduced himself, and informed Tommy that they were going to have a chat about how he was going to serve the *Hulder*, Bill had shown a marked amount of disrespect. He called Arend an upstart, an idiot and a man looking for a beating.

So, Arend merged a sphere of air with the gangster's left hand and, with a thought, caused it to exploded. The results were quite spectacular. Bill's hand turned into a mist of blood and bone chips, leaving a ragged, bleeding stump.

Both Mist and Remer had gone into such paroxysms of laughter they had to sit down to recover.

'Right, mister Little,' said Arend as he leaned back in the chair that had, until very recently, been Tommy Little's. 'I have a job for you. And by job, I don't mean you will be paid. Not as such, however, if you carry out my instructions in an appropriate and acceptable way, then I shall not reduce your cranium to the same state as that idiot's hand. Do you understand what I am saying to you?'

Tommy nodded.

'Are you sure?'

'Yes, sir. Do what you say or you gonna pulp my head.'

Arend smiled. 'Good lad, well put. For the gods' sakes, Remer, shut that moaning moron up,' yelled Arend as Bill let out a particularly loud squeal of agony.

Remer stood over the whimpering gangster, twirled his finger and then released a small fire-ball.

The sphere of burning plasma rocketed into Bill's left ear, sizzling and sputtering as it burned its way in.

This caused the gangster to give voice to a high-pitched wail of agony.

'Remer, stop playing with him,' snapped Arend.

'Sorry,' apologized the warrior mage as he used a gesture to explode the plasma. With a festive sounding pop, Bill's head disintegrated. Such was the heat of the fireball, there was little mess as the wound was immediately cauterized. Bill jerked spasmodically a few times and then went limp.

Mist leaned over the body and nodded. 'Neat,' she said. 'His head looks like an empty bowl.'

'Thanks,' preened Remer. 'Took a bit of control that. Nice to see it's appreciated.'

Tommy looked like he was going to faint. Up until now, he had always considered himself to be a hard man. Born and bred on the streets and fought his way up using violence as a tool.

But now he realized, he was a rank amateur. What he saw as violence, he now knew to be merely spirited high jinks in the scheme of things. Playground thuggery, as opposed to the true casually evil artistry that was happening in front of him.

'Tell me what I must do, Master, and please don't explode my head.'

'It's simple,' said Arend. 'I am going to commit a felony. There are some coins on the hundred-million-dollar wall that I wish to own. However, security is tight.'

'And they have guns,' interjected Remer.

Arend stared at his *Hulder* compatriot.

'What?' asked Remer. 'I didn't use dorky language. It's not like I said, Boom wands or Thunder sticks, I was just pointing out they were armed.'

'Remer.'

'Master.'

'Shut it. Now, as I was saying, mister Little. I am going to need a diversion. And a quite serious one at that.'

Of course, sir,' groveled Tommy. 'What were you thinking?'

'Explosions. Lots of noise. General carnage and mayhem. Most probably, strap a bomb to someone and get them to blow it up in the casino. That should detract any attention from the wall.'

'You mean, like a terrorist attack? That's not very

American, sir. And who would we get to do it. As far as I know, Jihadists are a bit thin on the ground in Vegas.'

'I wouldn't worry about that,' replied Arend. 'After all, you will be the one carrying the bomb.'

'Hold on,' blurted Tommy. 'No ways. I'd rather get my head exploded than my whole body. Not that it makes much difference in the end, admittedly. But killing all those innocent people. I don't think so.'

'As I already stated,' contained Arend, unabashed at Tommy's refusal. 'Don't worry about it. You will be doing it, regardless. Because, you see, mister Little, you shall have no choice in the matter.'

And the Master mage recited one of his more powerful spells, gesturing with both hands while doing so.

Tommy decided this was most probably the best time to make a break for it, what with the whole, becoming a human bomb thing in his short-term future.

But as he tensed his muscles, preparing to leg it, a waterfall of purple and red motes of light cascaded down on him. Some of the particles burned like fire, others juddered like electrical energy, and some sent ice cold waves rippling through him.

At the end of the light show, he was frozen. Unable to move a muscle. Even his eyes were stuck staring straight ahead. He could breathe, but that was it.

'We call that spell, the *Dominopupa*,' said Arend. 'In human speak I suppose it might translate as, Puppet Master. Basically, it means you are now enslaved to me. Utterly and completely. For example, raise your left leg.'

Tommy complied.

'Raise your right hand, and make it into a fist.'

Again, instant compliance.

'Now punch yourself in the mouth until I tell you to stop.

Tommy proceeded to beat the crap out of himself while Arend watched dispassionately, and Mist and Arend once again went apoplectic with mirth.

***

Tommy Little was no longer living it large.

Instead, he was standing in the center of the casino, some sixty yards from the Hundred-million-dollar-wall, wearing a long linen coat and sweating like an elephant seal in a sauna.

He was utterly exhausted. Not only from the constant terror of having being turned into a human bomb, but also from his repeated attempts to break the Puppet Master spell and run away. But every time he tried, he failed. Plus, he had now developed such a vicious migraine that he almost welcomed his imminent demise. Almost.

Tommy wondered what the bomb strapped to his torso was made of. It was the size of an A4 piece of paper, but maybe an inch thick. Didn't seem to

craig zerf

have any wires leading to it, nor did it smell like C4. Most likely, it was some weird spell driven thing that these evil, non-human heathens had put together.

He felt like weeping. Only yesterday he had been a king. Okay, a king of an admittedly crappy fiefdom, but now he was about to become a pile of human hamburger. And that truly sucked.

He wondered if he would go to heaven. After all, notwithstanding the odd torture. And murder. He was still a Catholic boy. He even went to church, sometimes. Okay, once, for his sister's wedding.

So, maybe.

The bomb thing went beep.

Then boom.

Tommy looked around him. He appeared to be standing in a cave. Darkness all about. The air redolent with the stench of brimstone.

'Where am I?' he asked.

'I'll give you a hint,' rumbled a voice that sounded like fingernails scraping down a coffin lid. 'You're not in Heaven.'

At that same exact moment, Arend had just opened a portal and he, Mist, and Remer, were leaving Las Vegas and transferring themselves to a nearby private airfield.

They had taken the three silver *Triginta* sestertii.

But they had left the rest of the currencies. And the remains of mister Tommy Little.

Because what happens in Vegas stays in Vegas. Or something like that. Arend never really understood the saying.

Now Belikov had ten coins.

CHAPTER 40

'I had truly forgotten how unbelievably stupid Orcs are,' sighed the Morrigan.

Balor shrugged. 'Try dealing with trolls.'

'Trolls are simple,' said the Morrigan. 'That is different to stupid. They are well aware of their limitations. Orcs, however, are so dense, they think they aren't. And that is true imbecility.'

'True,' admitted Balor. 'But be wary of true stupidity. It is unshakable. Like granite, it is hard and resistant to attack.'

The Morrigan snorted. 'We will see about that. How do I challenge these morons?'

'It's easy, simply walk into their camp. They will do the rest. And don't worry, I shall be right behind you. As shall my Fomorians.'

The Orcs were a nomadic species. Not for them the daily grind of growing crops and tending cattle. They left that to the lesser beings. Then they simply took it away.

War was everything to an Orc. It was the only way to prove one's worth in their society. It was the only way to feed your family and to gain respect.

To an Orc, battle was akin to shopping. You

wanted an item; you took your shield and mace and went and got it.

And contrary to many of the current versions of Orcs and Orcish society, the females of the species do not participate in these battles. Unlike the men, who are built like brick outhouses and possessed of a similar intellect as said long drop, the females are slighter, almost delicate, and twice as bright. Which is to say, still dumb, but not terminally so.

But even the females topped the Morrigan by at least a foot in height and a couple of hundred pounds in weight. The males were over four times her size.

As opposed to her usual, Old Hag visage, the Morrigan had assumed her comely young girl appearance. She wore a figure-hugging red dress, the sides slit to reveal shapely legs. On her feet, light leather sandals. In her hair, a matching red, silk ribbon.

Her only concession to combat, was a short Gladius strapped to a leather belt that hung loosely over her hips.

'Listen up,' she shouted as she approached the camp. 'Who's the head honcho? I demand The Right of Conquest.'

There was a flurry of movement as Orcish heads popped out of tents, warriors stopped sparring and women stopped carrying. They all turned to stare at the insane human who had entered their camp and challenged their chief.

A particularly large Orc exited one of the tents,

threw back his head and roared.

It was impressive. Loud enough to shake the very earth they stood upon.

'You dare challenge, Zogarth?' he bellowed. 'You just weak girly human. Zogarth strongest of strong. He smashes you to small puddle of squishy stuff, no problem.'

Zogarth swung his mace high and battered the ground with it in a demonstration of his squishing capabilities.

'Yes, very impressive, big boy,' scoffed the Morrigan. 'I demand The Right of Conquest; do you accept the challenge?'

Zogarth howled with laughter. Genuinely amused. 'Is no challenge. Is stupid. But I accept stupid girl's stupid thing.'

The Morrigan shook her head. 'Lot of stupid's in that sentence, Zogarth. Including the one shouting at me. However, regardless of whether you consider it a challenge or not, the lore states you have to accept, or forfeit. Now, if you are afraid of me, I understand. You can simply forfeit your right and I will gain control of your warriors. What say you?'

'Zogarth laugh at silly girl. Ha. And even ha ha. I accept worthless stupid challenge.'

He hefted his shield onto his left arm, adjusted his grip on his massive mace and stepped forward into the open area in front of his tent.

By now, most of the encampment were gathered around, more puzzled than excited. After all, why was this tiny human in a red dress committing suicide by Orc? Humans were very strange.

'Hey, Crow Woman,' shouted Balor. 'Make a show of it. And don't use magic. It's forbidden.'

The Morrigan sneered. 'As if I need it.'

Zogarth opened with the classic Orcish overhand blow, mace screeching through the air as he looked to crush his opposition with one fell swoop.

The Morrigan stepped aside without any visible effort, drawing her Gladius as she did. Then, with a casual flick, she opened a deep cut in Zogarth's right forearm.

The Orc reacted by whipping his mace sideways, seeking to smash the Morrigan's feet out from under her.

Instead, she leaped lightly over the weapon and, with another deceptively casual flick, opened a wound on Zogarth's chest, the razor-sharp short sword slicing easily through the Orc's leather armor and deeply into his pectoral muscles.

The huge Orc looked puzzled more than worried. He glanced briefly at his mace and then his shield, as if to check they were both still there, then, in true Orcish fashion, he swung for the fences once more.

The Morrigan ducked and let the mace whistle harmlessly over her head.

And again, the Gladius snaked out and bit deep. This time she plunged it into the back of Zogarth's right leg.

A few of the Orc's applauded the move, stomping their horny feet and banging their maces against their shields.

'Stop clap little girl,' shouted the chief. 'She no can defeat Zogarth. Me is too good. She just lucky stupid.'

'Enough with the stupid, you bone headed mouth breather,' quipped the Morrigan as she spun around and sliced a chunk of flesh from Zogarth's left shoulder.

From that moment on, the battle degenerated into an extremely violent, bloody, carnival sideshow.

Zogarth attacked. The Morrigan slid out of the way and carved pieces off the lumbering giant warrior. Rinse and repeat *ad nauseum*.

After twenty minutes, Zogarth stood still. He could no longer raise his arms and blood streamed off him like he was in a devil's shower room. His leather armor was in tatters, and his flesh hung off him like a beggar's rags.

The rest of the Orcs had stopped cheering and applauding. Now they simply looked on in silence. Zogarth's leadership had been tarnished to such a depth that even if he survived this contest, he would no longer be welcomed in the tribe.

What Orcish lore lacks in fairness, it makes up for in harshness.

'Little girl too hard to hit,' pointed Zogarth. 'She like buzzing fly with little spiteful knife.' He went down on one knee. 'Time for lucky girl to finish it. Put silly knife into Zogarth's eye. Make done.'

Without hesitation, the Morrigan stepped forward and did exactly as Zogarth asked. The Gladius punched through the Orc's eye with an audible pop. Then it continued on into his walnut sixed brain.

The Morrigan wiggled it about a little, for good measure, and then withdrew it and held the bloody blade above her head,

'I claim right of conquest,' she declared.

As one, the Orcs fell to their knees.

CHAPTER 41

Quinton lowered his rifle and looked up from his prone position. 'Half minute of angle,' he said with a slight smirk. 'Now that's what I call shooting.'

He was referring to the fact he had just shot a grouping of under four inches at eight hundred yards.

Emily frowned.

'What?' asked the legionnaire. 'You not impressed?'

'We don't go in much for long distance shooting,' replied Emily. 'The vamps move too fast for any shot over a few yards away.'

'Not when I'm shooting,' said Quinton. 'Hey, that's why you hired the experts. We can't all pull off shots like that.'

A couple of his men chuckled. They knew he was being cocky, but it was exemplary shooting. And their Commandant was known for his sniping prowess.

Emily held her hand out. 'Reload and pass me the rifle.'

Quinton raised an eyebrow, ejected the empty and slotted in a new, full thirty round box mag.

Then he handed the FAMAS G2 rifle over.

'You want me to shift?' he asked Emily.

Emily shook her head. 'No, I'll shoot off-hand.'

This time one of the men laughed openly.

Emily didn't react, she simply brought the rifle up to her shoulder, sighted and fired. Three shots a second for ten seconds.

She nodded to herself. 'Nice weapon,' she said. 'Great balance.'

She handed it back to Quinton.

The legionaries stared open mouthed at the target. In the exact center there was a ragged hole, perhaps an inch in diameter. Probably a little smaller.

'I said, we don't much go in for long range shooting,' she said. 'I did not say we couldn't do it. Now, gentlemen, the reason I am here is to take your training to the next level. I know you have just finished two weeks of hell with Master Ben Chu, and he says, in his words, you lot are the toughest sons of female dogs he has ever come across.'

She allowed the legionnaires their chuckles at that.

'But now, Tag, Muller, Troy and I, are going to show you how to kill vampires.'

Tag stepped forward, high stepping slightly as the snow was about a foot deep. 'How we gonna do this, girly?' her asked.

'Who are your best at hand-to-hand?' she asked Quinton.

'Besides me, Jacques, Stefan and Jefferson.'

Emily picked up a rucksack, opened it and took out three machetes. The eighteen-inch blades glowed subtly in the weak winter sun.

'Silver plated,' she said as she handed one to each of the men Quinton had nominated. 'These are often our preferred weapon against the *Nosferatu*. Particularly when we get close. They do significant damage, particularly as they are silver coated, they never run out of ammo and never jam.'

'We have been trained extensively in most forms of knife fighting,' interjected the Commandant.

Emily nodded. 'That's good. Now, you three, attack Tag. Do not hold back. Try your very best to do him harm.'

None of the men moved. Instead, they looked at their Commandant, their expressions a mixture of confusion and disbelief.

'But he is not even armed,' said one of the men.

Quinton shrugged. 'Hey,' he said. 'I'm your Commandant, but Emily is your leader. So, the next time she gives you an order and you hesitate, or look to me for confirmation, I swear on my word as a Legionnaire, I will tear you a new asshole. Understood?'

'Yes, sir!' shouted the legionnaires in perfect unison.

As one and without further ado, they attacked Tag.

It was three on one. And apart from their obvious numerical advantage, the legionnaires were well trained, fit, fast, strong and all were veterans of many close combat situations.

Tag used his new-found speed to dodge almost all of their efforts, stepping and weaving and turning. But they were good. Very good.

Eventually, one of the machete's found its mark, slicing deeply into Tag's right shoulder. Blood sprayed from the wound as the big man dropped and rolled away.

Sensing an advantage, the legionnaires redoubled their efforts, stabbing and swinging with deadly concentration.

But to their enormous surprise, they saw Tag's deep wound heal over almost instantly.

At the same time, Emily called out to him. 'That's enough,' she shouted. 'Quit messing around, we're here to see you fight, not dance.'

Tag grinned.

And shifted up a gear.

That was when the legionnaires realized the big man had simply being toying with them. His speed increased geometrically and what was fast become a mere blur of movement. Fists and elbows struck out, noses were bloodied, eyes blackened and, after a few seconds, all three of the attackers lay on the snow.

Tag held their machetes in his left hand.

He was still smiling.

There was a murmur of disbelief amongst the soldiers.

'Tag,' said Emily.

'Yes, ma'am.'

'You are extremely fast.'

'Yes, ma'am.'

'Too fast for those legionnaires, it seems.'

'Yes, ma'am.'

'Are you faster than a vampire?'

Tag shook his head. 'No, ma'am. Not even close.'

Emily turned to face the soldiers. 'Now you have an idea what we are up against.'

'How do we beat them?' asked one of the men Tag had just downed. 'No one can fight anything that fast.'

Emily smiled. 'Ask your Commandant. He killed a couple.'

The men turned to look at Quinton.

'Tell them,' said Emily.

'I anticipated,' said Quinton. 'They were too fast for me, so I just figured where they were going to be, instead of reacting to where I thought they were.'

'And that's how you do it,' said Emily. 'It's part skill, part guesswork and part luck. Sometimes, you just got to roll the dice when you're fighting these monsters.'

'Is that what you do?' asked Quinton.

Emily shook her head. Then she moved. It was like trick photography. Smoke and mirrors. The snow whirled up in a mini tornado accompanied with a thunderclap of moving air.

And the Shadowhunter was standing behind the Legionnaires. Some twenty feet away.

Then, with another explosion of movement, she

was back where she started.

There was a chorus of muttered cuss words and a general shaking of heads,

'Well, I guess we're not in Kansas anymore, fellows,' quipped Quinton. 'So, we're slow, weak, don't miraculously heal and we can't use our fire-arms because the vampires can dodge bullets. I must be honest; I'm beginning to wonder what we can bring to the party.'

'Don't belittle yourselves,' said Emily. 'After we've trained you and equipped you, you will be able to take out any vamp you want. It's all about technique and experience. For example, I didn't say you can't use firearms, I merely said, you got to wait until you can see the whites of their eyes. Or red, as the case may be, Then, when you get real close...'

Emily drew her two Desert Eagle .357 magnums, drew a bead on a tree some seven feet from them and pulled the triggers.

The custom magazines held nine rounds each, and Emily cranked them out at almost six a second. So, in just under two seconds, using both pistols, she hammered eighteen rounds into a two-inch circle on the tree.

'.357 rounds, silver tipped, custom mags, full compensators and suppression.' She replaced the magazine and handed one to Quinton.

The Commandant hefted the pistol a couple of times, aimed at the tree and cranked off a few rounds.

Then he grinned. 'I like.'

'And that is just a small sample,' said Emily. 'We got auto shotguns, grenades filled with silver shrapnel, UV lights, Holy Water, although that only works for Muller. Loads of stuff. And we will teach you how to go hand-to-hand with the blood suckers as well. Just because you are human, does not mean you are weak. Trust me.'

'I do, ma'am,' said Quinton. Then he brought his fist to his chest in a salute. 'Command us. We are yours.'

'Thank you,' said Emily, returning the salute.

The rest of the legionnaires followed suite, slamming their fists against their chests and crying out in union.

'Honneur et Fidélité pour Emily.'

Honor and fidelity.

They were telling Emily – their loyalty, their honor, and their lives, were hers to command.

CHAPTER 42

A shaft of burning plasma scorched through the air and impacted with the side of the mountain. A geyser of steam billowed up as the snow instantly hit boiling point.

'That is awesome,' yelled Quinton. 'It's like an artillery strike. Do it again. Shoot those trees.'

Grannus shook his head. 'I'm out. One shot, that's all. Back in the day I could do crap like that for hours. Now, not enough worship for more than one, maybe two a day. Anyway, what you got against those trees.'

'Nothing, just a target. Could just as well have been those rocks over there,' answered Quinton.

'Boy, you some sort of biophobe? You hate nature?'

'No, sir,' responded Quinton with a puzzled look. 'Not at all. Just picking out inanimate objects to blast.'

'Well don't,' said the god. 'Hey, do you want some shiny things?'

The Commandant shook his head. 'No thank you.'

'Heathen,' snapped Grannus as he turned and

walked away.

In the background, Tag, Troy and Muller were taking the rest of the legionnaires through some close combat training.

'Keep moving,' shouted Troy. 'To pause is to die. Never stop. And be unpredictable. Do not follow set combat moves, do not use prescribed combinations. Mix. Match. Drop, roll, jump. Use your elbows, knees, heads.'

The three hunters all carried six-foot-long staffs, *ala* Master Ben Chu, and they used them to swat any soldier who stopped moving as they sparred against each other.

'Hey,' yelped Jacques as Troy smacked him across the back of his head. 'What was that for?'

'Hesitation.'

'Less than half a second,' argued Jacques.

'A vamp can tear your throat out in less than half a second,' said Troy. 'He can strike you six times in a fraction of that time. You hesitate, you die. Now carry on.'

'Sir,' shouted Jacques as he continued fighting.

Troy grinned at Tag and Muller. He knew they were being harsh, but the hunters were actually hugely impressed with the legionnaires. They were tough, well trained and pushed themselves to the limit at everything they did.

As a result, they were improving faster than the hunters thought possible.

Merlin wandered over. 'Where's Emily?'

'She took the Prof and they're setting up some

sort of magical firearms training run,' answered Troy. 'You know, a combat alley, but with magic instead of pull up targets and springs.'

The wizard watched for a few minutes while the hunters continued punishing any soldier that paused or was too slow.

'They're good,' he commented.

'Very,' admitted Troy. 'How's it going with the gods. I see Quinton was trying to do some team training with them. He said he wanted to form a god-squad. Like a super attack team.'

'It's an absolute disaster,' answered Merlin. 'Mind you, I knew it would be, but sometimes it is best to let someone learn the folly of their ideas by themselves.'

'Why, what's going wrong?'

Merlin chuckled. 'You have to ask why four worship-hungry, egocentric, hyper-powerful beings can't play well together? To a god, the height of teamwork is not destroying another deity's followers. Asking them to participate in a fire-and-movement exercise while attempting to minimize collateral damage, is like asking a starving Pitbull not to eat a pound of dropped hamburger.'

In the distance Troy heard a loud bellow, followed by the sound of a tree falling.

'Ass on a stinking stick. Fore,' shouted the voice.

'Ah, that would be Belenas,' observed Merlin. 'He's using his hammer to smash trees down.'

'Why?'

'He says it's training, however, I suspect he's

doing it to upset Grannus. Grannus likes trees.'

A massive windstorm blew up in an instant, smothering Belenas in tons of snow. The wind was closely followed by a jet of steaming water, redolent with the smell of sulfur, that melted the snow away.

'And, now Latobias and Sirona have joined in.' He rubbed his temples with his fingers and sighed. 'I'd forgotten how much I hate working with deities. Really, it's like trying to control a bunch of hyperactive toddlers.'

'Hey, what's with the gods messing up the mountainside?' asked Emily as she walked over, her arm linked with the Prof's.

'Idiots,' shouted Merlin, throwing his arms up and storming away.

'What's got his goat?' asked Emily.

The Prof chuckled. 'He hates working with the gods, it's just been a while and he forgot.'

'Will they be of any use?' asked Emily.

The Prof shrugged. 'They hate the *Nosferatu*. How they react, that is anyone's guess. But if pushed I would have to say, on balance, they should do more good than harm. So, yes, they will be a help, most likely in ways you would never expect.'

'And that's about all we can ask for,' noted Emily. 'Hey, guys,' she continued. 'After you've finished hitting the legionnaires with sticks, I would like to give them a bit of rapid-fire weapons training.'

'Might as well,' said Tag. 'I wanna go and help

Belenas knock down trees.'

'I wouldn't recommend that,' advised the Prof. 'Unless you want a jet of water up your … umm … well, just don't.'

'Come on, soldiers,' commanded Emily. 'Time to go shooting.'

There was a collective sigh of relief as the legionnaires stopped pummeling each other. A few of them rubbed ruefully at the welts left from the oak staffs.

They formed up and followed Emily, marching together and singing in cadence.

Dans la brume la rocaille
Légionnaire que vous combattez
Malgré l'ennemi, la balle de raisin
Légionnaire, vous gagnerez.

Emily translated in her mind.

In the mist and over the mountains, and through the enemy's cannon and shot. We are legionnaires and we will win.

'Oorah!' she muttered to herself.

***

'Full auto,' said Emily. 'Always full auto.'

'Difficult to control with full auto,' noted Jacques.

'Yes,' admitted Emily. 'But it's full auto or die. You have to fill the vamp with silver, it's the only way to bring them down using a firearm. And you need to practice quick reloads. Fire, swop out empty mag, reload. Must happen in under a third of a second. I know it sounds impossible, but it can be done.'

'We're just human,' said Quinton.

Emily chuckled. 'No, you're not,' she said. 'You are Legionnaires.'

'*Valeur et discipline*,' the men shouted in union. 'Valor and discipline.'

'We drink, we fight, we die,' returned Quinton.

Emily nodded. She liked the way the legionnaires thought. It reminded her of the Pack motto. *To live is to suffer. To suffer is to live.*

'Right,' she shouted. Reload. Let's do it again.'

***

'One can never say a unit is perfect,' said Emily as she sat at the table. 'But my boys are as close as any humans could get.'

'Your boys?' questioned Troy with a slight smile.

Emily nodded. 'My legionnaires.'

'Piles of hairy dog snot,' yelled Belenas, who was sitting opposite her. 'Stop trying to crack walnuts with your hammer.'

'I like cracking walnuts,' returned Grannus.

'You're making walnut paste, not walnuts,' noted Sirona. 'And you're just conjuring the nuts out of fresh air, so why don't you just conjure up ones without shells. After you've hit it with your hammer there's nothing left. You can't eat that.'

'Don't want to eat it,' snapped Grannus. 'Got a

nut allergy.'

'Well why are you making walnuts?' asked Latobias.

Grannus shrugged. 'I like hitting them with my hammer.'

'That's it,' shouted Merlin. 'Enough. Any more of your petty bickering and you will have to answer to me.'

Belenas stood up and bellowed. 'You dare to threaten a god?'

'Obviously,' replied the ancient wizard.

No one spoke for a while.

Then the god of being depressed, shrugged. 'Fair enough.'

The rest of the gods laughed loudly.

Merlin sat down and rubbed his eyes with the heels of his hands.

'Gods,' he said. 'I hate them.'

'You'll be happy when it comes to the killing part of this whole adventure,' said Sirona.

'And the getting to places really quickly,' added Latobias.

'You know something,' interjected the Prof. 'I've been thinking. I'm not sure we're going about this the right way. Maybe, instead of finding vampires to kill, we should be seeking out the *Triginta*. That way, we can ensure Belikov does not get his hands on it.'

'Fine,' agreed Merlin. 'You can do that as well. Grannus, you're the god of shiny things. You know much about the *Triginta*?'

'Sure,' answered the god. 'Haven't heard any-thing about it for a few hundred years, but I'm sure if I put my ears to the ground, I could pick up something.'

'Great, help the Prof. Meanwhile, I'm going to bed before you lot make me wish I wasn't immortal.'

The team mumbled their goodnights as Merlin left the room.

tracting the ire of the Winter Queen.'

'The Winter Queen is an amoral bitch,' snapped the Morrigan. 'We would literally have to decimate her followers before she took action.'

'It will be a fine line we tread,' said Balor.

'Perhaps,' conceded the Morrigan. 'We shall have to ensure we tread it with care. Plus, the plan has the added advantage of allowing us to train our troops in readiness for the final battle with the Daywalker and her friends. Now, if you are quite finished with your belly-aching, do you think we could destroy this village?'

The gathered Orcs lit their torches, and the fire-light reflected off the snow and highlighted their steaming breath. Like fire breathing dragons.

The village guards, who had thus far been ignorant of the hundreds of Orcs waiting silently outside their walls, immediately sounded the alarm, ringing the bell next to the gate.

The Morrigan raised her sword and then brought it down together with her command.

'Attack!'

The horde ran forward, storming the village gate. Six of the largest carried a roughly fashioned battering ram. No more than a tree trunk with most of the branches hacked off.

They slammed into the gate, tearing it off its hinges and hammering it back into the village.

Although the gate was well made and sturdy, it was meant to keep wild animals out. And maybe the odd vagrant. But never an army of trained

Orcs.

Ululating and screaming and grunting, the Orcs spread through the sleeping village. The inhabitants began to respond. Some running out wielding rusty swords, or pitch forks or hoes. Some with mere sticks.

The massive Orcish warriors cut them down with ease.

The Morrigan strode in after. Balor walked next to her.

His Fomorians, terrible, monstrous ogre-like creatures, formed a wall of protection around the two of them. The Fomorians carried savage, rudely smithed weapons. Ten-foot-long bastard-swords, massive iron clubs with a forest of ten-inch spikes at the head. Shields that were simply huge slabs of iron.

And they projected before them an aura of absolute evil and menace.

Balor watched the slaughter with a slight frown. Particularly when children were being slaughtered.

The Morrigan sneered at him. 'What? Too bloody for you? Are you sure you have the strength of character to continue along this path? Or would you rather go back to your current state of near hibernation?'

Balor growled his displeasure at the Morrigan's scorn. 'Watch your mouth, crow woman,' he snapped. 'I am known as Balor the Smiter. Or Balor of the Evil Eye. Not Balor the child killer. There is no glory in this.'

The Morrigan shrugged her indifference. 'No,' she agreed. 'There is not. But that is a mistake made by many. They think war is glorious. Full of trumpets calling, and deeds heroic. That is untrue. Mostly, war is simply fear, and death, and screaming, and crawling in the mud, praying to your god that you be spared. I should know, war is my very existence.

'But later, there will be glory. Trust me, this is a means to an end, not the end itself.'

The Morrigan watched on as one of the Orcs squealed, an arrow seeming to magically sprout from his eye. Another two went down in quick succession. There was obviously an archer of some skill in the village. Most likely the village hunter.

'Find the archer,' shouted the goddess of war. 'And bring him to me.'

Two of the ten Fomorians split from the group and lumbered in the direction the arrows had come from.

The archer rose from behind an upturned wagon and fired at them, his hands moving so fast they were a blur. Arrows thudded into the Fomorian's armor and shields. Finally, one slipped past their defense and struck the one monster in the neck. But the creature didn't even flinch as he ripped the arrow out and continued forward.

The archer was skilled. And he was brave. But once Balor's Fomorians closed to within melee distance, it was all over in seconds.

craig zerf

The one who had been struck with the arrow unleashed a massive overhand strike with his sword.
The ungainly blade connected with the archer's
head and carried on downwards until it struck the
ground, savagely bisecting him.

Neither Fomorian reveled in their one-sided victory. In fact, they didn't even acknowledge it, they
simply turned and lumbered back into formation.
Job done.

The Morrigan was impressed.

It took almost an hour to reduce the village to
a state of post-apocalyptic ruin. What wouldn't
burn was smashed down. Bodies and body parts
lay scattered randomly about the area. Men,
women, children. Even pets and livestock. Orc bat-
tle-lust was difficult to stop. Once they got the
smell of blood in their nostrils, it was pretty much
all go until either they, or the enemy were dead.

However, the Morrigan had managed to keep
two villagers alive. An elderly couple.

Now, they cowered in front of her. She had not
bothered to have them restrained in any way. They
were completely harmless. But she reckoned their
age made them perfect witnesses and vehicles to
pass on her message. Old enough to garner some
respect, but not old enough to be considered mentally incompetent.

'Now, Fred and Ginger,' said the Morrigan. 'Listen
to me, and listen very closely.'

'Umm, that's not our names,' said the old man.

'Do I look like I care?' snapped the Morrigan. 'Do

you want to live?'

They both nodded frantically, their heads wobbling about on thin necks like balloons on a stick.

'Then do as I say. We are going to leave. When help comes, I want you to pass on this message. *To the Wizard and the Daywalker – look closely. This wanton death and destruction is your fault. Only you can stop it. With love, Morgan le Fay*. Repeat that.'

They both did, talking in perfect unison.

The Morrigan nodded. 'Good. I am pleased. If I hear you relayed that message even slightly incorrectly, I will know, and I shall be back. And then it's no more mister nice guy.'

She turned on her heel and strode away.

Balor, his Fomorians and the massed Orcs followed.

They left the three dead compatriots the archer had killed, lying on the ground. Orcs had no respect for the fallen. They saw them as failures.

Balor said nothing as they marched away. But a small part of him wondered if this new ally of his was perhaps a couple of sandwiches short of a picnic. Her obsession with Merlin and the Daywalker was most definitely on the wrong side of insanity. Not that he cared, it was merely a casual musing.

The horde marched off into the night.

CHAPTER 44

'The village of *Scharzesblut*,' said Merlin.

'Black Blood?' translated Emily. 'Who the hell calls their village that?'

'It's not as ominous as it sounds,' explained the Prof. 'We are in the Black Forest, and the village is famous for making *bludwurst*, or blood sausage.'

'And the fact that there's a massive *Nosferatu* owned castle looming over the village is just a co-incidence?' questioned Troy.

'Strangely, yes,' confirmed the Prof.

'So, I gather the plan is to go inside the dog bothering castle and exterminate the stink-breath blood suckers,' interjected Belenas.

Merlin sighed. 'Belenas,' he answered. 'We have been over the plan a dozen times. We break up into four separate attack groups. Troy goes in first to do a short recce, we follow when he contacts us via his link to Emily. Each group proceeds to their des-ignated area and they take it from there.'

'It's way too ass creepingly complicated,' said Belenas. 'My plan is much better. Less to go wrong. We walk up to the front door, smash it down, go in and kill everyone. Simple.'

'As much as I hate to, I agree with laughing boy,' said Grannus. 'Door down, enter, smash everyone's heads in, home for dinner.'

'Agreed,' said Latobias as he opened a portal.

The castle doors were plainly visible through the shimmering circle of light.

'Piles of poo to the *Nosferatu*,' bellowed Belenas as he charged through the portal, swinging his huge hammer around his head.

The rest of the gods followed.

'Damn it,' cussed Merlin. 'Idiots. Come on, let's go.'

Tag ran through first. 'Wait for me and missus Jones,' he shouted.

Emily, Muller and Troy followed, then the legionnaires and, finally, Merlin and the Prof.

Belenas swung his hammer into the door, smashing it off its hinges. With a bellow, he ran inside the castle.

'Pull the drapes down,' yelled Muller. 'Any that you see. Let's get as much sunlight in here as possible.'

A crowd of people came running down a huge sweeping stairway that rose from the middle of the entrance hall. They were armed with a variety of weapons. Shotguns, pistols and even swords.

Sirona blasted them with a jet of steaming water, causing them to crash into each other and fall down the stairs. As they piled up at the bottom, Belenas started playing whack-a-mole with their heads, crushing them with quick swings of his hammer.

Grannus joined in, except he simply stomped on them, breaking bones and crushing flesh with his boots.

Latobias summoned a whirlwind and pushed it down one of the corridors that led into the entrance hall, the whistling wind was accompanied by sounds of furniture breaking and then a chorus of screams.

A door at the rear of the hall slammed open and another bevy of armed familiars rushed out.

Tag hoisted his minigun up. 'Sorry, guys,' he shouted 'Missus Jones's dance card is full.'

The gatling gun squirted out a stream of silver coated lead. Tag wanted to conserve his ammo, so he only gave a brief two second burst. Two hundred rounds tore the familiars apart, coating the floor and the walls in blood and worse.

'Split up, you dog bothering gumdrops,' shouted Belenas. 'We can do more damage that way.'

With that, he sprinted up the stairs, and the rest of the gods followed, splitting up as they reached the first landing.

'This is not the plan,' said Quinton. 'What should we do?'

'Three teams,' answered Emily. 'Let the gods do what they want. Then, Quinton, you come with me. Pick three men to join us. Troy, you take three legionnaires. Tag, Muller, you get the remaining three. I'll go through the middle of the castle, cover the rear and anything we come across on the way.

Troy, take the left wing. Muller, you guys take the right.

'We clear the bottom, then proceed to the next floors and tidy up after whatever those nutcases are doing.

'Merlin, I can't speak for you and the Prof. What will you do?'

Merlin raised an eyebrow. 'Oh, I think we shall just remain here for a while. Keep ourselves in reserve.'

'Sounds good,' agreed the Prof as he took out his pipe and filled it. He offered his tabaco pouch to Merlin, and the wizard took it and began to fill his pipe as well.

'Right guys,' said Emily. 'Let's move.'

***

'Where the vamps at?' asked Tag.

Muller shrugged. 'There's more familiars than we're used to,' he said. 'And no food. They're probably in the dungeon with the grinders. Or maybe in one of the towers.'

'Food? Grinders?' asked one of the legionnaires.

'They keep human prisoners to feed on,' explained Tag. 'And a Grinder is like a messed-up vampire. One that went wrong during the turning. Still fast and strong and stuff, but a bit wonky. Like a rabid dog. The blood suckers keep loads of them. Vamp attack animals. They usually have to be locked up.'

More armed familiars poured out of a doorway.

Missus Jones barked at them. They died.

'That is one serious machine you got there,' commented one of the legionnaires.

'Yeah, we got a good thing going,' replied Tag.

Far above them, in the upper floors, the team could hear explosions, and the sound of a storm. Thunder, the crackle of lightning. And, right on the edge of hearing, Belenas shouting.

'Go lick a duck, you blood sucking shitake mushrooms.'

'Sounds like they found some of the vamps,' noted Muller.

'That Belenas is one nutty character,' commented Tag as he kicked in another door and hosed the room down with hot lead.

***

Troy assumed his wolfman form and took point. The three legionnaires in his fire-team followed him, their automatic shotguns at the ready.

A human familiar sprung out of an alcove and fired. The bullet took Troy in the shoulder, but the handgun round barely penetrated his hide. He dispatched the miscreant with a casual backhanded strike that removed the top of his head, along with most of the contents of his skull.

There was a dull plunk as Troy's regeneration ejected the pistol slug, dropping it to the stone floor. Seconds later, he was completely healed.

Another door burst open and two more familiars exited, firing wildly as they did. Slugs ricocheted off the stone walls, buzzing spitefully past them. The legionnaires returned fire, their shotguns booming loudly in the confined space.

And that's when the vampire struck. Dropping down from a beam on the ceiling, he landed on one of the legionnaires and, before anyone could react, tore his throat open.

As the blood sucker leaped to strike the next soldier, Troy moved.

The two supernaturals slammed into each other like a pair of wrecking balls. Claws and teeth and fangs and fists struck hard and fast. Blood arced across the room and the soldiers clutched at their ears as the roars of the wolfman and the shriek of the vampire filled the air.

The two remaining legionnaires were unable to help. There was no way they could draw a bead on the vamp, both he and Troy were moving too fast for the human eye to follow. To the soldiers, the battle seemed like a blur of movement, interspersed with howls and screeches and spurts of blood.

Then, as swiftly as it had begun, it stopped.

Troy stood over the vanquished vampire, holding its severed head in his right hand.

Casting it down he turned to the legionnaires. 'Come on, reload, get ready. We will return for your compatriot's body. Stay vigilant, this is just the beginning.'

***

'Guys, I should be on point,' said Emily.

'No,' responded Quinton.

The rest of the legionnaires nodded.

'What if I ordered you to let me take point?' asked Emily.

'I would have to respectfully ignore you,' answered the Commandant.

Emily looked at the three other legionnaires and saw the same look in their eyes. They were hers to command, unless they thought her order would put her in danger. Then they would politely ignore her.

'We have sworn ourselves to you,' explained Quinton. 'Now, you are our life. Our reason for living. You will not die before us.'

'Look, guys,' said Emily. 'I'm almost unkillable. It just makes sense if...'

'No,' interjected Quinton. 'We serve. We protect. I take point, Jacques, Stefan and Jefferson take flank and rear. You stand in the middle of the hard diamond.'

Emily shook her head, but she smiled at the same time. 'Okay, boys,' she said as she summoned Deathwalker. 'Let's roll.'

Quinton stalked ahead. He carried a Saiga-12 fully automatic 12-gauge shotgun with a detachable 20 round drum magazine. The double aught rounds were silver plated for maximum effect against any vampires

On her right, Jacques sported a Milkor 40mm

auto-grenade launcher. Six 40mm grenades loaded with a combination of silver ball bearings and silver-nitrate powder. As an area effect weapon against the *Nosferatu,* it was deadly. Actually, it was pretty effective against any opposition.

On her left, Stefan toted a SAW light machine gun. 200 round belt loaded with silver jacketed 5.56mm Nato rounds.

On her six, Jefferson. He carried two FN P90's. Compact submachine guns that used the new hypervelocity 5.7 x 28mm round.

The boys were loaded for bear. Super strength, Godzilla sized bear.

She hoped they were good enough to survive.

Quinton opened fire, churning out a trio of shots at someone hiding in a doorway. The man went down without a sound.

A clatter of running footsteps echoed down the hallway and a group of familiars came sprinting around the corner, firing as they came.

Emily and her team dropped to the floor and the Legionnaires opened up. The volume of fire was so great it literally tore the advancing familiars to shreds.

There was a brief lull as the men reloaded.

Then Quinton stood up and took point again.

Emily was impressed. They had reacted quickly with little fuss, and they had stopped firing as soon as the opposition was vanquished. All good.

They continued forward, clearing each room as they did.

After twenty minutes, Emily had to admit to herself – she was bored. She was so used to being on the cutting edge of every attack that these legionnaires treating her with kid gloves was actually staring to irritate her.

She wanted to get in on the kill, and although she realized that was not really the correct way to think, she didn't care. Both her and Deathwalker needed to fight.

She was Shadowhunter.

She was Daywalker.

She was Pack.

She was Warrior.

Finally, they reached the end of the interminable corridor. A set of iron bound oak doors barred the way.

Quinton swopped out his magazine for another loaded with solid slugs. Then he lined up the shotgun and burned off six rounds, blowing the lock off and forcing the doors open to reveal three obvious vampires standing in the middle of the dully lit room, fangs glinting as they bared their teeth.

Emily smiled.

Time to have some fun.

But before she could react, the legionnaires opened fire. Sweeping torrents of grenades, shotgun rounds, 5.56mm machine gun rounds and hypervelocity FN slugs.

It was as if a wall of fire was sweeping the room. And the shooting was controlled, almost every round striking their target.

In the first few seconds, over 500 rounds of ammunition and explosives tore into the vampires. Such was the concentration of silver coated lead that all three of the bloodsuckers were decapitated, their heads literally exploding into red mist.

Again, as soon as the team had finished, they reloaded. Then they stepped forward to check the bodies.

'They're dead,' snapped Emily. 'You can tell because you shot their heads off. That's usually a real obvious tell.'

Quinton stared at Emily for a few seconds. 'Have we done something wrong?' he asked, his expression one of concern.

Emily took a deep breath. 'No,' she admitted. He had done his job perfectly; it wasn't his fault that her dark side needed to spill blood. 'Well done, guys. Good job.'

The soldiers grinned. Happy. They had pleased their mistress.

Quinton was about to continue their search when the entire castle shuddered from a huge explosion. The ground shook, dust fell from the ceilings and the sounds of glass shattering and wood splintering echoed through the building.

Emily had no idea what caused the explosion, but she knew, it was huge.

'Head for the entrance,' she yelled. 'We need to talk to Merlin and regroup.'

As one, the team headed back the way they had come.

CHAPTER 45

The entire left wing of the castle was a smoking ruin.

'What the hell?' yelled Emily.

'These idiots blew the place up,' said Merlin, gesturing at the four gods.

'Had to,' said Belenas. 'Was full of snot licking vampires.'

'Hold on,' said Emily as she ran her eyes over the team. 'Where is Troy?' She turned to the gods. 'If you have hurt Troy, I swear, gods or not, you are all dead.'

A wave of coercion rolled out of her.

But the gods shrugged it off.

'No need for that,' grunted Troy as he emerged from the rubble. He was carrying one of his legionnaires. A second limped beside him. There was no sign of the third.

'Where is Bart?' asked Quinton.

Troy shook his head. 'Sorry.'

'The explosion?'

'No. Vampire,' replied Troy. Then he turned to Merlin. 'What happened? We were lucky to get out alive.'

'Blew the place up,' said Grannus proudly. 'Wasn't easy, I tell you. Not in our current reduced states, but we managed it.'

'How?'

'Sirona filled the whole floor with water. Then I hit it with a beam of superheated light, turned it to steam. Steam expands, boom! Then as it exploded, Latobias combined the explosion with a few lightning bolts and that was all she wrote.

'Belenas did nothing,' continued Grannus. 'Just complained about how depressed he was. Idiot.'

'Up yours, you malarking fart knocker. God of shiny things, pah! Pathetic.'

'What about the prisoners?' asked Merlin.

'What prisoners?' responded Grannus.

'Exactly,' shouted the wizard. 'You didn't even check. If there are human prisoners, and they were in the tower, you just murdered them all.'

Grannus looked shocked.

'I didn't murder anyone,' said Belenas. 'Remember, I just stood and watched.'

Troy held his hand up. 'You can stop worrying,' he said. 'There were no prisoners in the left wing. I would have smelled them.'

'You can smell the difference between a familiar, a vampire and a prisoner?' scoffed Belenas.

Troy looked at the god and growled. The sound was so menacing that Belenas took an involuntary step backwards.

'I am Omega,' said Troy by way of an explanation.

'Of course he can,' interjected Emily. 'He can smell emotions, sense fear, hear a feather drop from a hundred yards away. His senses are superlative. Differentiating between a vampire's familiar and a terrified human prisoner is comparatively easy.'

'Where are they then?' asked Merlin.

Troy sniffed the air a few times and then pointed. 'There. Underground.'

'Grinders?' asked Tag.

Troy shook his head. 'They were all in the left wing. A series of rooms under the tower. They wouldn't have survived the explosion. Even a Grinder will get squelched under a million tons of rubble.'

'Okay, let's get the prisoners,' said Emily. 'Latobias can fly them to safety. Even if he has to make a few trips. Then we need to go back to the hideout and figure out how, or even if, we can all work together in the future. Because this operation was, to put it bluntly, a steaming pile of crap.'

Emily headed towards the prisoners. Quinton, Jacques, Stefan and Jefferson immediately formed a hard diamond around her.

Troy raised an eyebrow and Emily grinned at him.

CHAPTER 46

Hadad sat back in his chair and lit his pipe. Soon the air was redolent with the fragrance of sherry and vanilla from the flavored tobacco.

The philosopher was concerned. The Blood King, Belikov, had just concluded his meeting with the heads of the other Russian houses.

When Belikov had insisted Jebe summon them and bring them to the meeting, regardless of what they wanted to do, Hadad had known it would result in bad feelings.

But Hadad had not been prepared for the utter hatred the other heads of houses felt for the Blood King.

Or their depth of disgust about the alliance he was suggesting. Nay, not suggesting, ordering them to be part of.

They did not believe the houses should be under one ruler. Autonomy was a multi-thousand-year-old tradition amongst the houses. To be held under one vampire's rule was an anathema to them. It was quintessentially un-*Nosferatu*.

But even though their rebellion bubbled close to the surface, none openly opposed Belikov. Because fear trumped their other feelings.

Then Belikov addressed them.

And for the first time, Hadad saw the power of the *Triginta*. Even though Belikov possessed but one third of the full artifact, his powers of persuasion, his charisma and his obvious leadership had been enhanced to the point of magic.

It took all of Hadad's tremendous intellectual prowess to resist the hyperbole, the persuasion and the all-enveloping influence Belikov was wielding. The *Triginta* turned his every proposal, his every utterance into words of silver and gold.

He was their Champion, and they were his disciples.

The Messiah of blood.

He had talked of the rise of the *Nosferatu*. How they would assume their rightful place on the planet.

Master of all.

Subservient to none.

They would rule, and the food would quiver in fear at the very thought of them.

Then Belikov had left the room to the sound of cheers and applause.

However, Hadad noticed that very soon after Belikov had left, the sway he held over them started to fade. And by the time the heads of the houses were leaving, their thoughts were once again reverting to what they had been prior to the Blood King's speech.

This was obviously because Belikov possessed

only a part of the full *Triginta*. If he ever managed to collect all thirty pieces, there would be no stopping him.

And that is what worried Hadad. In fact, it terrified him. He knew that the best way for the *Nosferatu* to survive was to remain in the shadows. To control the dark and leave the light to the humans. Feed, but do not attempt to subjugate.

Do not waken the sleeping giant. For in his insane desire for power and glory, Belikov had forgotten, the human's default setting is war.

And they are many of them.

Hadad knew, to war against humanity was to die.

With a frown he took a snuff box from his jacket pocket.

It was a small, shabby wooden box. Nothing ornate about it. A simple steel clasp, and a carved letter H.

He opened it carefully and looked inside.

There, resting in the bottom of the box, its tarnished surface covered in black, ground tobacco, was a single silver Roman Sestertii.

Even if Belikov managed to find the rest of the *Triginta*, he will never have the complete set.

And the ancient vampire smiled, for he knew, this was just the beginning.

FINI

Well – there we have it. Another chapter in

Emily's endless battle against the *Nosferatu*. I sincerely hope you enjoyed it.

If not, as always, please feel free to contact me and tell me why. Or, if you enjoyed it, it would be great to hear from you. Reviews are also nice – but seriously, don't feel obliged. I know they are a hassle.

zuffs@sky.com is my personal e-mail.

If you have like the Emily books – please take a look at my other series' – there are loads of them.

Here is a link to my author page on Amazon – if you like, you can hit the follow button. That way, you will be kept up to date on any new books, but you won't have to put up with any personal emails etc from me.

https://www.amazon.com/Craig-Zerf/e/
B0034Q97JW/ref=dp_byline_cont_pop_ebooks_1

Likewise – if you follow this link (or just look me up on Facebook) then you can hit like or follow there. Same result – info without hassle.

https://www.facebook.com/craigzerfauthor

Thanks again, guys. As we used to say back in the seventies (yes, I am that old) – *Keep your feet on the ground and reach for the stars.*

Emily will be returning in book 7 – WAR

And here are a few pages to whet the appetite…

EMILY SHADOW-HUNTER – BOOK 7

WAR

CHAPTER 1

The Duke of Wellington once said – Nothing except a battle lost can be half so melancholy as a battle won.

This is just a posh British way of saying – war is crappy, even if you win it. But losing one is even crappier.

The windrows of dead villagers had not even had the privilege of fighting a battle. They had simply been exterminated. Smoke rolled across the remains of the burned-out buildings. Corpses lay strewn like so much flotsam and jetsam.

Some lay alone. Others in clusters. Whole families, lovers, friends.

Together in death as they were in life.

A dog gnawed at the single Orcish corpse one of the villagers had managed to kill.

Flocks of hooded crows, rooks and ravens darkened the skies as they came looking for carrion. Foxes and badgers slunk through the deserted streets, stopping every now and then to tear a chunk of flesh from one of the fallen.

Then the sky clouded over and, within seconds, it began to rain. Heavy, sullen drops of water. Like the heavens were weeping.

A woman stood alone in the center of the village green, surrounded by the end of her life as she knew it.

Her eyes were dry, because she was past lamentation. Past desolation. Past everything but achieving the mere basics of life.

Breath in.

Breath out.

Even the thundering sounds of galloping horses approaching did not cause her to move her head. She simply stood.

Her mind as empty as the nothingness left of her existence.

Everyone she knew was dead.

Finally, she looked up, her attention focusing on the detachment of upper Fae cavalry that had just pulled up in front of her.

One of the Fae nudged his steed forward, stopping right in front of her.

The commander of the detachment was one, Lord Jingo Partridge. A leader known more for his relative closeness to the Winter Queen than his military prowess.

'You,' he called out. 'Peasant woman. What happened here?'

She looked up at him, her face a mask of absolute subjection. 'They're all dead,' she whispered.

'I can see that, woman,' snapped the commander. 'Who did this?'

The woman blinked owlishly and then spoke,

her voice bereft of emotion. 'There is a message,' she mumbled. 'For the Daywalker and the Wizard. Only you can stop this. Love, the Morrigan.'

Lord Partridge stared at her, his face a picture of bafflement. 'What does that mean?' he shouted. 'Explain, peasant.'

Ignoring the lord completely, the woman looked about her, then, slowly, she shambled over to one of the fallen. Bending down, she picked up a small dagger that had fallen next to the corpse.

Without warning, she placed the blade against her neck – and slit her own throat.

'Bloody hell, woman,' yelled lord Partridge. 'What you go and do that for? Idiot, I still had questions.'

As he was raving, one of the other cavalrymen dismounted, walked over to the woman and checked her pulse.

'Sergeant Pillory,' snapped Partridge. 'What the hell do you think you're doing?'

'Just checking, my lord,' answered the sergeant.

'She's obviously dead,' said Partridge.

'Seems that way, my lord,' agreed the sergeant. 'I shall organize a team to ensure she gets a decent send off, sir,' he continued. 'We will gather all of the villagers and construct a pyre on the east side of the village.'

Lord Partridge waved his hand dismissively. 'No need,' he said in a bored tone. 'I'm sure the crows and the foxes will take care of the carrion. Leave it, we need to report to the Queen.'

Sergeant Pillory pointedly ignored his commander and ordered six of his troops to dismount. 'Carry the bodies to the east wall,' he instructed them. Then, turning to the rest of the squad he told them to collect enough wood for a funeral pyre.

Finally, he turned to face lord Partridge once more. 'The pyre will be set as you instructed, my lord,' he informed his commander. 'I am sure the Queen will be very impressed at the compassion you have shown her loyal subjects.'

Lord Partridge stared at the non-commissioned officer for a few seconds before his self-importance and inbred sense of entitlement overwhelmed the obvious lack of obedience being shown him.

'Yes, sergeant,' he agreed. 'Make it so. I shall be outside. Send some of the men to set up an awning and chairs and table for me.'

Sergeant Pillory bowed deeply.

'It shall be done, my lord.'

Only when the aristocrat had ridden back through the village gates did the sergeant allow his distaste show. And only for the briefest second.

Then he turned to oversee the sad and gristly task of preparing the villagers for their funeral ceremony, at the same time wondering who the Daywalker and the Wizard might be.

CHAPTER 2

Merlin's face was pale with fury. His eyes shone with emotion and his breath came in short jagged inhalations. Like a man in pain.

'Calm down, my friend,' said the Prof. 'You'll do yourself no end of stress damage going off like this.'

'Calm down,' yelled Merlin. 'Easy for you to say, it isn't your name that is being tied to literal genocide.'

'How many?' asked Emily, her face as pale as Merlin's. 'How many have they killed?'

Merlin shrugged. 'Not sure. Hundreds? Not thousands.'

'Not yet,' interjected the Prof.

'Well, we have to stop it,' stated Emily.

'It's a trap,' said Troy.

'Obviously,' agreed Emily. 'But that doesn't matter, does it? Innocents are dying. And they are dying because of me. It has to stop.'

'Not because of you,' said Grannus. 'Because of that insane crow woman.'

'She is doing the killing,' admitted Emily. 'But the dying is because of me. I am ultimately responsible.'

'Not true,' interjected the Prof. 'I would say that, ultimately, Merlin and I are responsible. After all, we showed mercy, of a sort. We imprisoned her instead of destroying her essence. So, the blame lies with us.'

'Hey,' said Tag, his voice raised almost to a shout. 'Enough. Seriously, enough whining about whose fault it is, or isn't, or might be. Me and missus Jones say, let's go get this bitch.'

'What he says,' added Troy.

Merlin stood still for a while, thinking.

'What are we waiting for?' asked Emily.

'Pause for a while, child,' replied Merlin. 'Obviously something needs to be done about this. However, it will do us no good rushing in without a plan. Or without knowing what the long-term consequences might be.'

'The long-term consequences are that innocent people will keep dying until we show up,' stated Emily.

'Fine,' returned Merlin. 'So, what do you suggest we do? Open a portal to the world of the Fae, rush in where angels fear to tread and then what?'

'We find the Morrigan and stop her,' replied Emily.

'How?'

Emily frowned. 'I don't know,' she admitted. 'But surely it's better than sitting on our asses while people are dying.'

'No,' denied Merlin. 'It isn't. Look, I understand,

more than you think. I have witnessed countless vile acts such as this. Death beyond imagining. And if there is one thing I have learned, going off half-cocked will only result in failure. So, stop. Think. Approach this from a place of calm, not anger.'

Emily took a deep breath and nodded. 'You're right,' she said.

'How about I make some tea?' asked Tag. 'We can discuss it all over a nice cuppa.'

'No tea for me,' snapped Grannus. 'Booze is what I need. Whoever heard of the god of shiny things drinking tea?'

'In all fairness, shiny thing guy,' returned Tag. 'No one. But that's only because no one has heard of you, period.'

'Are you taking my name in vain?' bellowed Grannus.

'No,' replied Tag. 'All I is saying, the god of shiny things don't sound so cool. Maybe, back in the day when peeps wore animal skins and stuff, shiny things was cool. Now, not so much.'

Grannus was about to reply when, instead, he hesitated, thinking. 'You mean, I need to change with the times?'

'Exactly,' agreed Tag. 'For a start, god of shiny things sounds lame. What you need to be is – the god of Bling.'

'Bling?'

'Yeah.'

'What the hell is, Bling?'

'Hold on,' said Tag. 'Before I make the tea. Look at this.'

The big man took out his cell and did a quick search of the internet. Then he held the screen up so Grannus could see.

'Who is that,' asked the god.

'That be Mister T,' replied Tag. 'See all those gold chains and shiny jewels? That be Bling.'

'The god of Bling,' mused Grannus. 'I like it. Yes. From this day forth, I, Grannus, shall be know as the god of Bling.'

'Right on, man,' cheered Tag.

'But still, no tea,' added Grannus. 'Booze.'

'Sure,' agreed Tag. But trust me, you don't know what you is missing.'

CHAPTER 3

The portal crackled open with a flash of lightning and the smell of ozone. Slowly, it widened until it was both wide enough and tall enough to fit two people side by side.

Latobias strode through, followed closely by Sirona, and Belenas.

The team were working on the theory – if you are going to enter a potentially hostile environment, send the gods in first. Grannus had stayed behind to follow up on the *Triginta*.

'Well, we're in the pox-ridden, donkey farting right place,' noted Belenas as he turned back to face the portal. 'All clear, you piles of monkey midden,' he yelled.

Merlin and the Prof came next. Then Troy, Muller and Tag.

Finally, the legionnaires, crowding in closely around Emily. Forming a human shield against any harm that may threaten her.

As the last one came through, the portal flickered closed.

Quinton gestured to his men and they fanned out to form a perimeter, weapons ready. Tag hauled missus Jones from his shoulder and scanned the immediate area for unfriendlies.

Emily noted a huge wall in the distance. 'What's that?'

'The capital of the winter realm,' answered Merlin. 'The seat of the Winter Queen. That's where we're heading.'

'Why we come out so far away? 'asked Tag. 'Couldn't we have popped out in front of the gates? I don't like walking much, seems unnecessary.'

'It's very necessary if you want to stay alive,' answered the Prof. 'Any portals opening within five miles of the walls get zapped. There are powerful runes spread around the capital and they are charged on a daily basis by top Fae mages.

'It's for security. Stop armies opening up portals and attacking. This way, you can only materialize a few miles away and then they see you coming, raise the alarm and ready their defenses. But at the same time, it is still close enough to allow important guests, trade missions and such, relatively easy access.'

'Makes sense,' admitted Tag. 'Well, let's get to walking then.'

The team began their five-mile trudge through the knee-high snow.

Both Tag and Troy grumbled as they walked, picking their knees up high to facilitate movement.

'Bloody snow,' mumbled Tag. 'Sick of snow. Next time we go vampire killing or Fae saving I vote we do it in Jamaica. Sun, rum and jerked chicken.'

'I'm with you, big man,' agreed Troy. 'I've seen about enough snow to last a lifetime.'

'I think it's beautiful,' disagreed Emily. 'The way the sun sparkles off the ice in the trees, the pristine whiteness of the landscape, like it's just been spring cleaned. It's amazing.'

No one answered, concentrating instead of merely putting one foot in front of the other. Their progress was slow. Slower than normal due to the fact they were all carrying vast amounts of ammunition and ordnance.

Each legionnaire carried his primary weapon and anything from a thousand rounds to five thousand rounds of ammunition for the same. Over fifty pounds of dead weight.

Three of the legionnaires were carrying the respective parts of a 60mm mortar as well as their primary weapon and ammo. Every soldier carried five rounds for the mortar, adding a further twelve pounds to their loads. Finally, they each carried ten M14 'toe-popper' anti-personal land mines. They weighed in at a mere three and a half ounces each and were made to maim, not kill. Perfect miniature force multipliers.

Apart from that, they carried little else. Water, a small medic kit each and a few MRE's.

Tag had gone large with his ammo, as he knew the prodigious rate missus Jones went through it. Fortunately, due to his inordinate strength he was able to hump a combined weight approaching five hundred pounds. That included ten thousand rounds of ammunition.

In short, the hunters had enough firepower to fight a war. Which was exactly what they were intending to do.

It took the team two hours to get to the walls, and as they got closer, Emily marveled at the sight. They loomed over them, vast and intimidating. The walls themselves were over a hundred feet high. Every sixty feet or so, a stone tower reared upwards, on the top of each, either an arrow throwing ballista or a mangonel catapult. Hundreds of archers lined the battlements and more guards were massed in front of the main gates. Cavalry patrolled the surrounds and one of the detachments approached them as they neared the walls.

'Are these guys fighting a war?' asked Muller. 'They definitely seem to be on a war footing.'

The Prof shook his head. 'No. Both Fae courts are big on showing strength. This level of preparedness is normal.'

'Okay,' interjected Merlin. 'here comes the cavalry, let me do the talking. Tag, did you hear me? This will call for subtlety and diplomacy.'

The big man nodded. 'Sure thing, boss man. I get it, subtlety and diplomacy are not my strong suite.'

'Shouldn't one of the gods do the introductions?' asked Emily. 'Surely that would impress the hell out of them?'

'No,' replied Merlin. 'The Fae follow strict proto-

craig zerf

col when it comes to deities. Unless there is a priest present, custom dictates they do not even acknowledge the god. Most likely though, they won't even realize that Latobias, Sirona and Belenas are gods. So, pipe down about that.'

The cavalry detachment pulled up in front of the team of hunters. Thirty strong, they formed a line barring their way. One of the men nudged his mount forward. His fancy uniform and the plumes in his headgear picked him out as the ranking officer. As did his expression of vague disdain.

'State your business,' he commanded.

'We are here to see her majesty,' answered Merlin.

The upper Fae nobleman sneered at the wizard. 'No chance,' he scoffed. 'Now, I might allow you to enter the city, if the requisite payments are made. And I say, might. But first, a few questions. What are those strange devices your servants are carrying?'

'Servants,' spluttered Tag.

'Tag,' snapped Merlin. 'What did I say?'

'Subtlety and diplomacy.'

'Good man,' the wizard turned to the cavalry officer. 'These are not my servants,' he informed him. 'And I am not under your command. So, sir knight, I suggest you get your men out of our way and allow me to enter the city in order for me to visit the Queen. I am on an important mission and have little time for self-important, low level horseback riders such as yourself. Now, begone.'

The Fae cavalry leader stared open mouthed at Merlin and then, with deliberate slowness, he drew his sabre. The blade rasped out of the scabbard with a chilling sound of metal against hardened leather.

But before it was fully drawn, Merlin mumbled an incantation, and then, with a gesture, lifted the Fae lordling from his saddle and threw him some fifty yards away. He landed with a dull thump in a deep drift of snow, the drift deep enough to save his life, but not deep enough to prevent a few broken bones and an inevitable loss of consciousness.

'Hey, maybe I can do this subtlety and diplomacy thing after all,' said Tag. 'Instead of magic though, I'd just use a fist.'

'Not sure how diplomatic that was,' ventured Troy.

'Or subtle,' offered the Prof.

'Shut up,' growled Merlin as the rest of the cavalry troop drew their weapons and started to advance on the team of hunters.

'Enough,' roared Latobias, stepping forward, flanked by Sirona and Belenas. 'I begin to find your attitudes irksome.'

He wove a pattern in the air and, with a heave of his shoulders, launched forth a howling blizzard.

Sirona conjured up a spray of water droplets that turned instantly to sharp shards of ice in the sub-zero temperature.

And Belenas rose his massive hammer high and

struck the frozen ground with such force it felt like an earthquake.

Within seconds, the horses had bolted or simply fallen down and the cavalry riders were scattered about on the snow, some unconscious, others nursing broken limbs, ragged ice-cuts and full-body bruises.

Fortunately, the company sergeant was still *compos mentis*. Because it is well known that, while the lords and commissioned officers hold the rank, the actual leading is done by the non-comms.

Because, as is oft quoted, sergeants run the army. The officers are simply there to give things a bit of tone and prevent warfare becoming a mere lower-class brawl

So, while the ranking officer lay broken and unconscious in a deep snow drift, the sergeant snapped to attention and threw the gods a perfect salute, despite the fact his right arm appeared to be broken.

'Begging your pardon, misters,' he bawled at paraded ground volume. 'We appear to have made an error. On behalf of the Winter Queen and my men, we apologize and beg we be allowed to escort you to the palace as you requested.'

'Good man,' replied Merlin. 'What about your officer?'

'I'm sure he will be fine, sir,' replied the sergeant. 'After all, his head is so far up his own ass I am confident he will not freeze to death. Now, if you would follow us. Well, us that can still walk, I shall present you to her Majesty.'

And so, the hunters entered the city of the Winter Queen, following a limping, horseless, broken and humiliated detachment of her majesty's cavalry.

CHAPTER 4

'Tell me, sergeant,' said the Queen. 'Where is lord Ponderberry now?'

'Unconscious at the bottom of a snowdrift, your imperial majesty, beckoner of storms, mistress of snow and guiding light of the Winter.'

'If he survives, when you see him next, tell him - by order of her Majesty, he is now a common foot soldier. His rank, his titles, his lands and his wealth are now yours. Kneel.'

The sergeant dropped to his knees.

There was a murmur of surprise amongst the gathered courtiers, but they made sure their voices were not raised loud enough for any possible dissention to be audible.

The Winter Queen conjured forth a sword of ice. Leaning forward in her throne, she touched the sergeant on each shoulder. 'What is your name.?'

'Reekus Mallington, your imperial majesty, beckoner of st...'

'Yes, yes. Enough,' interjected the Queen. 'I dub thee, lord Mallington. Now go.'

The sergeant – nay, the lord – stood, bowed and stepped back. He left the throne room, taking three steps, bowing, another three. Rinse and repeat until he was out of sight.

'Nice one, dude,' commented Tag as he watched the newly minted aristocrat retire. 'Nice to see a brother go up in the world.'

The Winter Queen glared at the team of hunters. But Emily noted that her imperial stare was marred slightly by a barely notable tic. The corner of her right eye betrayed the emotion she was hiding behind her mask of regality.

Particularly when her gaze rested on Merlin.

It was impossible to hide emotion from Emily. She could hear the Queen's heartbeat. She could smell her subtle changes in body temperature. She could see the tiniest of visual clues.

And she was only slightly shocked when she deduced that the emotion the Winter Queen of the Fae was hiding, was fear.

This imperial monarch of all around her was afraid of the wizard. But she was strong enough to conceal the fact from her subjects.

'What are you doing here, Myrddin Wyllt? Your presence always brings upheaval.'

'You well know what I am doing here, majesty,' replied Merlin. 'For even you are not so detached from your subjects as to not have knowledge of the current mass extermination that is currently taking place in your realm.'

'A few villages do not amount to genocide,' returned the Queen.

'Your concern for your subjects overwhelms me,'

replied Merlin. 'So, you are aware of it. I take it you have also heard the messages left with the scant survivors of the atrocities?'

The Queen did not answer.

'The Wizard and the Shadowhunter?' prompted Merlin.

Still, the Fae Queen remined silent.

'Listen Feliticia,' said Merlin, ignoring the horrified gabble that arose from the courtiers at his use of the Queens given name. 'Could we dispense with the whole game of thrones, subterfuge thing? Really, the machinations of the court make my teeth itch. We are here to put a stop to the needless killing currently being committed by the Morrigan and her allies.

'We all know she is only doing it to bring us to her, and so, here we are. This visit is a courtesy, not an obligation. We do not seek your permission; however, we do seek your blessing.'

'You do realize, I could have you all clapped in chains for merely thinking my given name, let alone addressing me by it,' stated the Queen.

'No, majesty,' corrected Merlin. 'You could try to have us clapped in chains.'

The Queen cast a look at her detachment of guards, as if to contemplate ordering them to do as she had threatened.

At the same time, the sound of weapons being cocked, clattered through the room. As did the low hum of Missus Jones's barrels spinning in preparation to open fire.

A wave of power rippled from the trio of gods as they too prepared for a possible confrontation.

Surprisingly, the Queen did give an order, but it was not what anyone expected.

'Leave the room,' she commanded her subjects. 'All of you, even the guards. I want to be alone with these people.'

The captain of the guard stood forward. 'But, majesty,' he began.

However, the Queen stopped his voicing with a mere look.

He snapped to attention and led his men from the throne room, ensuring all of the courtiers left as well.

The door swung shut behind them, closing with a hollow boom.

The Queen's expression changed, softening slightly, allowing her true self to show through.

'Your visits always bring pain,' she addressed Merlin in a soft voice.

Merlin shrugged. 'I come when needed. It is not my fault that usually I am only needed during times of disorder and upheaval. I did not bring the pain, I come to stop it.'

'Why is the Morrigan doing this?' asked the Queen.

'It is a personal vendetta,' replied Merlin. 'Against Emily and myself.'

'Emily?'

'The Shadowhunter,' stated Merlin.

Emily stepped forward and bowed slightly. 'Majesty,' she introduced herself.

The Queen blanched. 'Such power,' she whispered. Then she cast her gaze over the rest of the team. 'This is too much, Merlin,' she said. 'Even for you. You bring gods and supernaturals into my domain without so much as a warning. Are these who I think they are?'

'Depends who you think they are, I suppose,' answered Merlin.

'Latobias. Sirona. Belenas.'

The gods nodded their acknowledgment of the Fae Queen.

'Technically, I should not be addressing you personally,' continued the Queen. 'It should be done through the auspices of a priest. I hope I am not offending.'

'Ha,' scoffed Belenas. 'We didn't make that stupid rule. That was made by the church. Yet another way for them to gain more power. Deny access to the gods. Keep it all for themselves. Charge people to do what is actually their right. Thinking about it, maybe a bit of good old-fashioned smiting would sort things out. At least it might stop some of the corruption. Whatever, girl, you address us all you want.'

The Queen inclined her head. 'Thank you.' Then she turned to the rest of the team, singling each one out as she spoke.

'Professor.'

The Prof bowed.

'Omega.'

Troy held his closed fist to his chest in salutation.

'The Pious.'

Muller bowed.

'The Immortal.'

Tag chuckled. 'That's what they say, Queeny. How you doing?'

The Queen frowned, not sure how to take the big man's familiar style of greeting. She decided to ignore him and continue her perusal of the team.

'These humans,' she said to Merlin. 'I have not heard of them.'

'Legionnaires,' said Merlin.

The Queen nodded. 'Ah, yes. Romans. Who is their Centurion?'

Quinton stepped forward and saluted. 'That would be me, majesty. And not Roman. *Légion étrangère*. We protect the Shadowhunter.'

The Queen raised an eyebrow. 'I doubt very much the Daywalker needs much protecting.'

'Be that as it may, majesty, we have given our life to her.'

'Very well. Now, tell me, wizard, how do you propose to stop the Crow from murdering my people?'

'If I may, majesty,' interjected Emily. 'Why haven't you already sent out troops to stop her?'

'It is a fair question,' replied the Queen. 'Many reasons. Firstly, the slaughter has not reached endemic proportions. You must bear in mind; my realm is huge and I have many millions of subjects. The deaths of a few thousand mean little in the overall scheme of things.

'Not only that,' continued the monarch. 'The Morrigan has used the Right of Conquest to take control of several Orc tribes. As of this moment she has approximately six hundred Orcish warriors under her flag.'

'Surely that means little next to the size of your army?' insisted Emily.

'True,' conceded the Queen. 'However, I must be very careful lest things escalate. The Orcs, the goblins, even the Dwarves hover constantly on the edge of rebellion. If I use too heavy a hand, the lesser tribes may well use it as an excuse to revolt.'

'I see,' acknowledged Emily. 'But if we intercede that should be acceptable.'

'As long as I am not seen to be too involved,' added the Queen. 'I will however insist you take one of my representatives with you. He will be your guide as well as advisor as to our rules and customs.'

'I know your customs better than you do,' interjected Merlin.

'Be that as it may,' snapped the Queen. 'I insist.'

'Fine,' conceded the wizard. 'We shall leave tomorrow and head towards the last known incident. I assume we will be offered accommodation in the palace.'

'You assume much, wizard.'

'Yes or no, Feliticia,' returned Merlin.

'Yes. Of course,' sighed the Queen as she pulled a silken rope next to her throne. A quiet tinkle of a bell sounded outside the room. Instantly, the door opened and the courtiers paraded back in.

'You, lord Melberry,' commanded the Queen. 'Show these gentlemen to the eastern guest wing. See to it they want for nothing.'

The Lord bowed. 'As you command, your imperial majesty, beckoner of storms, mistress of snow and guiding light of the Winter.'

'One thing, your queenliness,' interjected Tag. 'Have you guys got French stew and long bread.'

The Fae Winter Queen stared at the big man; her train of thought totally derailed by one of Tag's classic non sequiturs.

'I ... what ... we...' she stammered.

'Never mind,' said Merlin as he grabbed Tag by the arm. 'Let's move.'

The hunters traipsed from the room, following lord Melberry's lead.

Domination (Emily Shadowhunter, Book Six) © 2021 by Craig Zerf

craig zerf

As always – to my wife, Polly and my son, Axel. You chase the shadows from my soul.